Tiny Bones

Rosemary Smith

INKWATER PRESS
Portland • Oregon
INKWATERPRESS.COM

Scan this QR Code to learn more about this title

Cover and interior design by Emily Coats
Trunk © Dario Lo Presti. Bigstockphoto.com
Beautiful woman in white dress © staras. Bigstockphoto.com
Old white window with bricks © studio023. Bigstockphoto.com

Publisher: Inkwater Press

Paperback
ISBN-10: 1-62901-201-7 | ISBN-13: 978-1-62901-201-8

Kindle
ISBN-10: 1-62901-202-5 | ISBN-13: 978-1-62901-202-5

Printed in the U.S.A.
All paper is acid free and meets all ANSI standards for archival quality paper.

1 3 5 7 9 10 8 6 4 2

Acknowledgments

Thank you to my husband, who has been forced to read more changes in more sentences than any man should ever have to endure. Thank goodness his mother is a painter and a poet, so he grew up with it and doesn't realize that other husbands don't have to do those things so often.

Thank you to all my friends and family who are patient with me during the times when I am busy writing. They do still call to ask about my health and ask me to lunch and sometimes I break away and go with them because even I know it helps to get away from the computer once in a while.

Thank you to all the good folks at Inkwater Press. Your help and your patience are a blessing. I am grateful that you have been there for me and have not pushed me to go faster during this particular book than I was able to go. I appreciate you all.

Prologue

Houses have personalities. Some have an aura of hominess the minute you walk in the door. Others seem embarrassed if they don't look their best and are thrilled when a potential buyer talks about making them look pretty again. You can feel it in the air. When some homes have suffered through tragedy or felt the touch of evil, they become tainted in a way that's hard to overcome. Paint and new carpet cannot hide the negative vibrations.

The house in this story was one of those. It sat on a hill beside a road in south Alabama for a hundred years. The peeling white columns across the front porch spoke of a time when cotton was king. You could still see the fingerprints of the slaves who made the red bricks.

Many people stopped by to look at the house, and a few dreamed of making it into a home again but something held them back. It could have been the faintest sound of a baby crying in the distance. It could have been the chill in the air when they stood in the second bedroom upstairs or the vision of a young woman in a lacy white dress reflected in the mirror hanging in the hall. It would take the right people, a lot of love, and plenty of hard work to make the house overcome the left-over emotions from what had happened a century before.

Chapter One

1882

Eloise Bledsoe leaned against the pillows in her narrow bed, running her hands over the cotton nightdress covering her swollen belly as she had every morning of the past few months. Carrying a baby in the summer could be quite uncomfortable but she liked feeling the baby moving inside her body. Sometimes she hummed a little tune as she caressed her tummy. The small morning ritual made her feel closer to the child. She picked up her stiff paper fan from the bedside table and tried to move the hot and humid air around a little for the both of them. It didn't do much good.

She whispered to the life inside her, "What do you look like, little baby of mine? Are you a boy or a girl? Can you hear my voice? Do you have dark eyes and straight brown hair like my own or is your hair dark and curly like your father's? It doesn't matter. I am going to love you so much. I already love you more than I would ever have dreamed possible."

She leaned forward, arched her aching back, and used both hands to wrap her lank brown hair into a bun on the back of her head, securing it with a couple of pins from her bedside table. The strong cramps had been coming for several hours and the baby was less active than on the past few mornings. There'd been one moment earlier when she could actually see the shape of a tiny foot pressing against her skin from the inside out. Seeing it made her smile and she touched the little foot and jumped as she watched it jerk back. At that moment, she realized the obvious. That little foot belonged to her child. Before too much longer, she'd be holding it, kissing it, and getting to know that little person. It was the strongest moment of bonding she'd felt since discovering her pregnancy. Her emotions were so high, she didn't know whether to laugh or to cry. And so she laughed with happy tears dripping down her cheeks.

As her hands traveled around her bulging middle, the muscles tightened and the process began again. The skin was stretched tightly over the smooth roundness and the whole mass was hard and felt full enough to burst. She rode the wave, instinctively taking a breath and blowing it out as the muscles contracted and finally began to let go.

That one was more painful than the one before and they seemed to be getting closer together. She hadn't watched the clock but was sure there was less time to rest between each pain than there had been when she felt the first ones in the wee hours of the morning. She wondered if she should send for Missy, the colored woman who would be acting as midwife, but decided to wait. There was always a chance that the pains would stop. There had been several times over the past few weeks when the pains had come and gone for a few hours and then disappeared completely. She figured Missy would be by sometime that day anyway and she would ask her about the pains when she came to visit.

One part of her mind was afraid. The night before, her mother had stood in the doorway of her bedchamber with her long black and silver-streaked hair flying from its nightly brushing and her hands on her broad hips, throwing hateful words at Ella by the mouthful.

She shouted, "The sin you have committed was a big one and you can expect the pain to be just as severe. God does not condone such wantonness. He will teach you a lesson, young lady, you can rest assured." She had turned on her heel and marched back to her own room, leaving Ella to hope with all her heart that her mother was wrong.

Rita Bledsoe wanted her daughter to confess all of her sins and especially to tell her the name of the man who'd caused this terrible thing so that he could also be punished. Her need for punishing seemed almost stronger than her curiosity, and she'd probably move heaven and earth if she could to accomplish her goal.

Ella said her morning prayers asking the Lord to be with her because she was afraid and had so many questions. She'd never even seen another pregnant woman up close and knew very little of what to expect, except for the gossip she'd overheard from the Negro women who worked for her parents around the house and in the fields throughout her life. She accepted responsibility for her sins and had asked God for forgiveness many times. She'd made a mistake because she was young and had allowed herself to be overtaken by feelings and sensations that she'd never before imagined to exist. She was paying a huge price. Even so, she felt a kind of peace and forgiveness from God, but she never expected it from her mother.

Rita Bledsoe was a woman grown cold as a stone, even before the death of her husband not long before her daughter's pregnancy was discovered. Ella was reasonably sure there wasn't any forgiveness left inside the woman.

Another part of her was glad her labor was finally beginning. It was time to get past the birthing and know if she had a daughter or a son. She wanted to be the best mother there ever was, in spite of the fact that she had no husband.

She hoped that in this child, she'd have someone who would belong to her alone, who'd love her and depend on her completely. For once, she'd know that she mattered to someone. She understood there would be a few difficulties, but she had to believe there would be good times too.

Sometimes she tried to imagine the sweet sound of her baby's voice as she played silly little baby games, but she had so little experience with small children that it wasn't an easy task. It was easier to think of them walking hand in hand after a few years. Often she pictured a boy and other times she'd see a little girl looking much as she did when she was younger. She wanted to spend time with her child and get to know it in ways that her parents never had taken the time to do when she was growing up. Her child would never be lonely.

She'd tried to think of names but finally decided to wait until the baby arrived, reasoning that she'd be able to find a name that fit within a day or two.

She'd been named after a long-dead relative and disliked her own name immensely. The only portrait she'd ever seen of the first Eloise hung in her father's study. The lady appeared quite dignified but with her hair slicked back, deep lines around her mouth, and a long, stiff neck buttoned up in a high collar, she looked tired and very unhappy. Ella used to stare at the portrait and often wondered if that picture was a glimpse of her own future. She certainly hoped it wasn't.

Her mother had already made it clear that she wouldn't be allowed to use the family names because she wasn't married. She meant to shame her daughter by making such a declaration, but it didn't bother the girl at all. She wouldn't have used any of those old-fashioned names anyway.

Ella thought the most important thing was to give her baby a good strong name of its own and let the infant know that it was cherished in spite of the circumstances of its birth. She'd read the word "cherished" in a book and liked the feeling of it on her tongue and in her mind. Just saying the word felt like a kiss. Cherishing seemed to involve a deeper kind of feeling than simple love, and she was determined to give her child the best kind of love that she could possibly give, complete with lots of hugs and kisses.

She was determined to find ways to make up for the illegitimacy. She planned to work at it awfully hard. Her own parents never said the word "love" very much, but Ella planned to use it often. Her son or daughter would never wonder where he or she stood in the emotional scheme of things. That was the reason she talked to the baby even before the birth. She felt it was very important to both of them and it was fun. She didn't know for sure if the baby could hear or understand her words but she enjoyed doing it anyway.

Another pain began and she moaned softly while holding onto the metal rails of the headboard, trying hard to think of the future and not to think about the pain at all. There was so much to learn about being a mother. There were so many things to do for a child. Surely, she would be able to manage it. Other women did it. Missy had promised to help her learn what she needed to know.

Ella got up from her bed and began her morning routine. She needed to wash herself and put on clean undergarments and a light cotton dress and then she'd go out to the kitchen to see what Slimmy had cooked for breakfast. She wasn't one to eat in her room unless she was ill. She liked sitting at the kitchen table and talking with Missy and Slimmy. Her mother didn't really approve but was usually in her own room until midmorning and would not know anything about what went on until she came out fully dressed in her stiff black mourning dress.

Over the past week, Ella had spent a lot of time thinking about how life would be for her child. She thought that a boy would have an easier time with some of the problems this particular child would have to face. Young boys were allowed more freedom. A boy would be able to go fishing or hunting with the men or older boys.

From her own experience, she knew the life of a daughter was not easy. Daughters were often ignored. There was never anyone for a girl child to talk to unless there were brothers, sisters, or cousins around. Ella had had no one to talk to since she was five years old. It had been a lonely existence, stuck as they were out in the Alabama countryside. A girl was stuck at home and limited to reading, sewing, and riding, unless she had a great number of friends to provide an active social life. Her mother spoke longingly of her days of attending reading groups or having tea with her friends. She said they'd talked of the newest novels or the latest fashions. Those things sounded dull to Ella. She enjoyed reading her father's newspapers and wished that he would discuss the articles with her. But he didn't. Even if she'd had a great mind, she wasn't encouraged to use it. No one was interested in hearing about her thoughts or ideas or even her biggest fears. When she did ask a question, especially about the farm or politics, she was usually told that she shouldn't be concerned with such issues. She thought, *Why not? A girl has a brain, doesn't she? Why couldn't a girl be interested in the same things as a boy?*

Judging from what she read and heard from her mother, it seemed that an active social life was primarily designed to find a husband. A girl was expected to become a wife and a mother. Ella had accidentally skipped the part about having the husband. It wasn't done by design. The truth was that having a husband didn't appeal to her much anyway, but she'd never admit that to anyone.

There was another part of her great sin that had not come to light as yet. That part would be harder on a daughter as well, and so she sincerely prayed for a son. Her mother and the aunts and uncles in Pennsylvania would simply have to understand and forgive her, if they cared for her at all. It had been such a long time that she wondered what they knew of her. Her mother wrote long letters to them all, but she had no idea what her mother said about them and their life in Alabama. There was nothing happening to write about unless her mother was pouring out her misery and wishes to be back there with all of them.

Ella barely remembered her relatives up north. They were just names of strangers mentioned in letters sent by her mother's sisters, and none made her react with melancholy the way they affected her mother. On the rare occasions that a letter arrived from her people, she would carry the missive in her pocket for days and read it over and over.

Ella had never had a letter of her own. Perhaps if she had, then she would understand.

Ella's only friends were her horse, Maggie, and her fluffy orange cat, Theodore. Theo was old and spent most of his time sleeping in the shade of the gardenia bushes in the garden. Sometimes Ella sat on a quilt spread on the grass near his resting place to read a book and to be close to something alive.

According to the rules of Rita Bledsoe, the few southern girls Ella had met in her own age group were not suitable companions because they were from different social backgrounds and some of them were colored. There was no way that a Bledsoe daughter would be allowed to have colored friends. The white daughters of the plantation owners were not interested in her friendship because her father was not a plantation owner, but only an "overseer," even if Mr. Bledsoe had not used the title. He preferred being called a Farm Manager. It was more dignified, modern, and less reminiscent of the days of slavery that were supposed to be over. Her family had never been invited to the parties at the big plantation house, nor were they ever asked to tea.

During her mother's tirade the night before, she had shouted, "It is a good thing your father was already dead when we found out this baby was coming, because the news that his only daughter had been with a man outside of marriage would have surely killed him."

Remembering those hateful words, she covered her eyes with her trembling hands and whispered, "Oh, Papa, I am so sorry to have done something that would have upset you so. I didn't mean to cause this problem for any of us. I wish that you were here to guide me."

Her father had been a man of strong religious convictions, but he was also very gentle and forgiving. She wanted to believe that he would have probably been upset with her at first, but eventually would have come around and understood that she had not done this thing on purpose. He surely would have been very angry at the man involved but would have forgiven her and done his best to make the situation turn out well for his daughter. She would never have told him her lover's name but he wouldn't have demanded it the way her mother did. Her father was never one to hold a grudge or hang onto anger. His Quaker beliefs would have given him a way to deal with it all. She knew that deep inside her heart.

Ella thought, if her family had stayed in Pennsylvania, she might have been able to learn the ways of her Papa's religion. His quiet and peaceful attitude matched her own nature much better than her mother's angry and demanding form of worship. Her few memories of sitting in her father's church were filled with soft voices and gentle words. The God that Ella spoke to in her prayers was a kind father figure, with a quiet demeanor. Even the Bible stories she liked best told about Jesus and his gentle strength. Her mother, however, favored the tales of God's punishment of sinners. She heard God as a judge with a loud thundering voice and pictured Him with an upraised fist.

Ella recognized that she had sinned. There was no way to get around it. Her life was not going to end up the way her parents had planned for her. Before this pregnancy, she'd never done much thinking about her future. She took life one day at a time and did the best she could to find some joy in everything.

Her parents had spoken of sending her back up north to stay with one of her aunts so that she could be introduced into polite society but her father passed away before any plans were set into motion. That would not be possible after the baby came, and she had no choice but to face the reality of it and make the best of the situation. There would be no fancy wedding in her grandparents' house. There would be no lace wedding gown or bridesmaids or wine punch to sip from tiny silver cups. But she would have her child and somehow that seemed all right. Her mother and her relatives up north would have to get used to that idea one way or another.

It was hot already. The clock on her mantel read eight o'clock.

Ella yawned and while stretching to her full length, felt a small rush of warm water from between her legs. She jumped to her feet quickly. At first she was aggravated, thinking that she'd wet herself, but quickly remembered the talk that she'd had with Missy a few days before about what to expect when she went into labor. She realized that the bag of water that held the baby inside her body had ruptured.

She grabbed up her cotton slip from the day before and used it to soak up the wetness. Missy had told her that once her water broke, it meant she was going into labor or would be soon. There would be no going back from that point. It was beginning. Her biggest secret would soon be out. Her mother was going to have a "hissy-fit," as Slimmy would say. She hoped that she could be physically and emotionally strong enough to handle it.

Poor Ella had been confined to the house for most of the last few months so that no one would know her shameful secret. It was like being in prison. She wasn't even allowed to walk outside or ride Maggie. After the baby was born, she would be free again.

Today I am going to become a mother, she thought to herself. It was a good feeling.

Chapter Two

Hobbling on bare feet, she stepped to the head of the stairs to call out for Slimmy, the kitchen girl. "Slimmy, I need you to get Missy for me, please. I think the baby is coming soon. Tell her that my bag of water broke. Hurry, Slimmy, please, I don't know what I'm supposed to do."

She turned to look down the hall and saw her mother watching her while buttoning her black crepe dress.

"Eloise, you do not yell like a field hand. Ladies must control their voices." She frowned at her daughter and turned back into her own room. Ella thought she looked like she was readying herself for battle. Seeing her mother did nothing to boost her confidence.

Slimmy nodded her head slowly and took her own time drying her hands on her apron, and smoothing out the wrinkles. She said, "I'm goin', Miss Ella, I'm goin' in jes' a minute. Don't you be worryin' none. Babies take their own sweet time, especially the first ones. There ain't nothing for you to do 'cept wait till it gets here. These things happen in the Lord's time and we all gotta wait." She added silently,

Even little spoiled white girls gotta wait and go through labor pains...jes' like ever'body else on this earth.

The screen door screeched open and slammed shut as Slimmy stepped across the small covered porch and down the three wooden steps. She followed the well-worn path to her cousin's house on the other side of the garden, stopping to pick a ripe tomato and sticking it into her apron pocket. *There is nothing better than a perfectly ripe tomato, I'm gone slice this one up to go with my peas and cornbread for dinner today,* she thought.

She figured there was no reason to rush. It would be hours before things got serious, so there wasn't any reason to run.

Slimmy didn't like carrying messages. She had better things to do with her time. It was funny that everybody talked about the changes that were supposed to come when they were all freed from the bonds of slavery, but the fact was that nothing much had changed in Slimmy's life. She'd been a house girl as a slave, helping in the kitchen and doing light housework, and that was pretty much what she did as a free woman too. She got a little money for doing it now, but her life wasn't that different at all. She'd have thought that she wouldn't have to work so much, but now there were things to buy like coffee, flour and sugar, and cloth for clothes, all of which she used to get for free from the Whittingtons. She'd never want to go back to being a slave, but then she was not inclined to work her fingers to the bone for a few pennies either. Life just wasn't fair somehow and she didn't understand it at all.

She climbed the rickety back porch at Missy's house and hollered through the open door.

"Missy, Miss Ella sent me to get you to come quick. She said to tell you that her water broke. I got to git back over there, 'cause I got things to do this mornin', ya hear?"

"Ok, tell her I am comin' in a minute. I'll be there as soon as I get Joe's biscuits outa the oven. Did she seem all right to you? Was she scared?"

"I don't know how she seemed, Missy. She was standing there in the door to her room in bare feet and she said to tell you to hurry a-cause she didn't know what to do. I don't know if she was scared or not. It ain't my job to know what's in that girl's head."

Slimmy started back down the steps and back from where she had come. She had chores to do at the Bledsoe house and she was not hanging around and getting herself into trouble with Mrs. Bledsoe just because a baby was coming. She hoped she wouldn't have to spend the whole day listening to that girl screaming and hollering. If she worked it right, she might manage to get the rest of the day off to get those string beans canned over at her daughter's house. They had a dozen new canning jars waiting on the kitchen table, and those beans would not wait forever.

Missy had everything she would need for the birthing within reach and had been waiting for the call. After looking up at the sky last night, she knew in her gut that the youngster wasn't going to wait past tonight. There was going to be a full moon. Lots of babies were born on the day or night of a full moon. She didn't know why that was, but it was true. Her mama had said it was all part of God's plan...another one of God's mysterious ways.

This is goin' to be a very long day, she thought to herself. *That young gal over there has been livin' a soft life and has prob'ly never known real pain in her whole sixteen years. She's bound to feel some today for sure. She's got herself a big ole baby in that belly of hers.*

When Missy had put her rough bony hands on that roundness to check things out the day before, she could feel the infant's strong kicking and moving.

It made her feel happy to feel a baby moving like that. Birthin' babies was a really good thing to do. It made her feel like she was doing God's work. This morning, she already said her special prayers and asked the Lord to go easy on the girl. Sometimes it helped and sometimes it didn't. Some of them had it easy and some suffered hard during the birth. Missy hoped for an easy time of it for all of their sakes.

She hoped there was a pot of coffee already made at the house. She hadn't even had herself a biscuit for breakfast. She'd been too busy getting ready, in case she got the call. She turned back, took three big brown biscuits out of the pan that she'd pulled out of the oven a few minutes before, wrapped them in a clean cloth, and set them on top of the stove to stay warm for her brother Joe, and took the pan with six others with her. Joe would have his breakfast after he got back from doing his morning chores out in the barn.

There ain't no point in goin' hungry, she thought. *Maybe Slimmy would have some ham or bacon cooked.* Mrs. Bledsoe did love her ham and bacon and often ate them for breakfast. Slimmy usually cooked a slice or two extra so they'd get a little taste for themselves. Mrs. Bledsoe didn't seem to mind. A meat biscuit and a pot of coffee would help things a lot. It might be the only meal she got that day.

She said another silent prayer as she gathered up the rest of her stuff and headed out through the garden patch. *Lord, I got me a bad feeling about this here birthin' and I cain't figger out why. That girl seems big enough and healthy enough but they's like a bad cloud hangin' up in my head and I just cain't get it to go away. You got to hep me on this one. But, then you hep me on all of them, don't you, Lord Jesus? I know that and I thank ye. I shore do wish Mama was here to hep us both. She was so much better at this healing stuff than me. But, we gone do the best we can, ain't we, Lord? Yep, we gone do the best we can.*

Missy shivered as she walked barefooted through the soft red dirt between the rows of the garden to reach the overseer's house. She hoped that she had the shivers because she was hungry and the bad feelings would go away as soon as she got herself a cup of strong sweet coffee and a bite to eat.

Missy got there just as another contraction began. Ella had been wringing her hands and pacing the floor of her room while waiting anxiously for her to arrive. The midwife closed the window, sat the girl on the little bench in front of her dressing table, stripped the bed, and covered the mattress with a sheet of oilcloth to protect it. She put clean cotton sheets on top of the waterproof layer so that Ella would be more comfortable. Missy could tell she was getting scared. She talked softly and helped the young woman back on the bed and propped her sitting up with a rolled-up quilt and some pillows. The girl did as she was told and sat there looking at Missy with big round eyes full of questions. She talked rapidly and in a high-pitched voice.

"Missy, is it going to hurt as bad as Mother says it will? Will it hurt worse for me because I am not married? Mother says that God is going to punish me. I hope the baby is going to be all right. Do you think it will be all right, Missy? God doesn't punish babies for the sins their mamas committed, does he? How long will it take for the baby to come? I hope it gets here fast. I can't wait to hold my child and see if it is a boy or a girl. Do you know how to tell if it is going to be a boy or a girl, Missy?"

"It's all in the Lord's hands, chile, all in the Lord's hands. If he be willin', then it'll be all right. We do what we can and we prays for the rest. That's about all any of us can do. Now, you jes' sit back and try to breathe easy. It's gone take as long as it takes. They ain't no way of knowing 'zactly how long that will be. We gone hafta wait and see. We gone hafta wait and see if it is a boy or a girl too. There ain't no way to tell. My sister says that if you take a sewing needle on a piece of thread and hold it over the mama's belly you kin tell. If it swings back and forth it is s'posed to be a boy and if it goes around in circles den it is s'posed to be a girl... or it might be the other way around, I cain't never get it straight. I don' put much stock in that kind of stuff. I just leave it up to the Lord. It don't make no difference anyhow. It is gone be one or t'other and you shore can't change it once it gets here, now can ye?" She gave a little laugh and poured some warm water in the wash bowl, brought it over to the bedside table, and told Ella that wiping her face with a wet cloth might make her feel cooler.

The words didn't bring Ella as much comfort as Missy had hoped. Ella couldn't sit still and wait. After a few minutes, she got up again and emptied her bladder in the commode chair beside her bed and then began to pace once more from one side of the room to the other.

Her mother came into the room and sat in the chair by the window to keep an eye on the proceedings. She said, "Eloise, get back in the bed and do what Missy tells you to do."

Ella held onto the bed frame and closed her eyes when another contraction hit and barely managed to sit down before her knees gave way. That was the hardest pain of any she'd had so far. A little moan escaped her lips and she made an effort to stop it.

Her mother said, "Eloise, you have not been in labor nearly long enough to be carrying on so. You are a woman now and pain is a woman's lot, especially in childbirth. Let this be a lesson in being strong. Women need to be strong. Stop whining and just do what Missy tells you and it will be fine."

Missy patted Ella's hand. "It's all right, Miss Ella, you can holler if you want to. Some folks say it heps them some to get through it. There ain't nobody here but us. It don't matter none at all if you need to holler."

Mrs. Bledsoe frowned and glowered at Missy but kept silent.

Ella didn't want to be one of those women who screamed and cried out. Her mother was right. She needed to be strong. Women had babies all the time. It was natural and if the rest of them could do it, then Ella figured that she could do it too. It was not ladylike to complain and her mother would surely remind her for the rest of her life if she disappointed her by making too much fuss.

Missy laid out the things from her bag and explained the purpose for each item to her patient. There were soft towels for cleaning up and a blanket in case the girl got cold, although that wasn't likely in the heat they were experiencing that summer. She had a clean sharp knife for cutting the cord after the baby arrived. There was another sharp pocket knife that she would put on a kitchen towel and slide under the side of the bed. Her mother had said that knife was there to spiritually cut the pain. It was another of those things that worked sometimes and sometimes didn't seem to help at all. She had a jar of hog lard for making things move easier if need be. She took the sharp pocket knife, whittled a piece of soft wood into a smooth stick about six inches long, and then wrapped it in strips of cloth she tore from a ripped-up sheet.

"What's that thing for?"

"It's for when things get bad. You gone need to bite down on it to hep you get through the pain."

"Missy, how bad will the pain get? They are hurting pretty bad now. I don't even want to think of it getting too much worse."

Missy looked her straight in the eye and told her the truth, "I done told you, I don't know, chile. It's bad for some and not so bad for others. That Ledbetter gal from down the road had one a couple of weeks ago that hardly bothered her at all. She was up cooking breakfast the next morning, so her mama told me. We gone jes' have to trust in the Lord and wait and see. You got wide enough hips, so maybe it won't be too bad. It's them little tiny gals with hips like a boy that's usually gone be the ones that has problems. You should do real fine. I'm prayin' it's gone come fast and that the pains will be easy for you. Don't you be spendin' too much time thinkin' about how bad it might get. Jes' take each one as it comes and then go on to the next. It'll be easier fer you if you don't think about it too much. I promise you that thinkin' about it ain't gone change a thing."

Ella tried to obey. She wanted to be good. She'd already disappointed her mother in so many ways.

Since she had no first-hand knowledge of giving birth or other womanly things, she had to place her faith in Missy's ability. Missy had worked beside her own mama, who'd delivered the babies on Whittington Plantation for many years, so Ella felt certain that Missy must have plenty of experience in those matters. Besides, Ella knew her mother was not about to call a doctor and risk letting people find out that she was having a baby without the benefit of a wedding, so Missy was the only person she could turn to, anyway.

"Come on now, Miss Ella, you jes' lay back on them pillas and take it easy while things are going slow. Womens been having babies ever since God made us and it'll be all right in the end. It's God's will. Yo mama is right about one thing. We ain't hardly even gotten started yet. You need to get some rest while you can. You gone need all your strength there toward the end."

The hours must have passed, but for Ella, time dragged. She grew tired and wondered why God made it so hard for children to be born. She thought that He should have made it easier so that people would look forward to the experience. Then she felt guilty for questioning the wisdom of God. She closed her eyes and tried to rest and hoped the next pain would be a long time coming, but it wasn't long at all.

Missy went out to the kitchen to find herself one of the biscuits she'd brought in earlier and to get a cup of Slimmy's coffee. She chose a nice thick slice of ham from the covered plate on the table to tuck between the two buttered halves of her biscuit. She chewed as she watched Slimmy wash up the breakfast dishes and then got up and dried them for her and put them in their proper places while Slimmy swept the floor with a broom. They'd cleaned that kitchen together many times and each knew the way to get it done.

Mrs. Bledsoe came to the kitchen door and asked how things were going. "Missy, will this thing drag on into the evening or will it be over before dinner?"

"Things is going about like we'd expect them to for a first baby. It'll probably get to moving faster in a couple more hours. But they ain't no way to know whether it's gone be past dinner or not."

Mrs. Bledsoe said, "Slimmy, after you get the kitchen chores done, will you put on a big pot of water to get hot? After that, you can go on home if you want to. There's no point in all of us standing around waiting for this to be over."

"Thank you, Ma'am. I will. I got some green beans that need canning over at Jeb and Nina's house and I could use the extra time. Missy, you want me to send one of the kids over from time to time to see if you need anything?"

"Thanks, Slimmy, but I think we gone be all right. I'm goin' to go sit with her for a spell. She's getting tired already and I want to try to get her to rest between the pains. I wish she'd give it up and try to sleep but she is all wound up and cain't find no peace."

Chapter Three

Ella's screams ripped through the fetid air like jagged knives made of sound. Missy and Rita Bledsoe cringed and tried not to hear them. Missy regretted saying that it was all right for her to holler. The girl had managed pretty well until noon but since then, she'd suffered through a couple of hours of hard labor and was exhausted. It was hard to witness someone else's agony. Both felt there wasn't much chance of seeing it finished before dinner.

The two older women stuffed the padded stick into Ella's mouth for her to bite down on and also to hush her up in case there was someone close enough to hear. Ella had forgotten all about being lady-like and yelled as loud as anyone Missy had ever seen. The girl's screaming made her worry that something wasn't going right. A certain amount of pain was to be expected but Ella was not the kind of girl to scream for nothing. If she was hurting that much, then there might be a serious problem somewhere. She wished that she knew how to make it go faster and be easier.

Mrs. Bledsoe rinsed out the rag and mopped her daughter's face between contractions and tried to give her comforting words. She decided that her daughter had suffered more than enough to pay for her sins. She began to fear that her harsh words about God's wrath might have given Him ideas and now she was sorry that she'd said those things. She began to pray for Him to take away some of the pain and let the baby be born as soon as possible.

Missy pulled back the sheets to see how the birth was progressing. She explained to them that things were going like normal and sometimes it could go on for as much as a day or more. She told them of one girl who gave birth to a baby girl after laboring for nearly two days. It already seemed like a long labor to Ella and she surely couldn't envision that kind of pain going on for two days.

The contractions came right on top of one another and didn't give her any time to rest in between. She was drenched in sweat and wished that she could climb into the big tin tub and cover herself with nice cool water and feel clean again and wash her hair with lavender-scented soap. Ella hated being dirty more than just about anything and this whole experience felt dirty and painful and miserable, and she was more than ready to see it end.

In spite of her words of encouragement, Missy still had the nagging feeling that something wasn't right. She went over her mental checklist and couldn't find anything out of order. The baby just wasn't moving down like it should. She had massaged the swollen belly and tried to make the girl relax so the baby could move down the birth canal, but Ella was very tense and nothing seemed to help. She wished again that her mama was still alive and there to help her through this situation.

Her mama had been the best midwife around. Everyone who knew of her said it was so. Missy wished, not for the first time, that she had been blessed with the gifts the Lord had given her mama when it came to healing and birthing babies. Missy cared a lot, but she didn't have the same natural talent or the special healing touch that her mama had. Some folks got blessed with it and some folks had to do the best they could with what they'd been given.

Ella squeezed her eyes shut, rolled her head back and forth, and held on tightly to the iron bed frame behind her, straining so hard that her face turned red and the veins stood out in her neck and forehead so they looked ready to burst. She had the beginnings of blisters on her palms and fingers from twisting them on the metal bed. Missy told her to let her body go limp so the pains could do their work, but Ella fought each contraction with all her might. She'd tighten up her whole body until it was rigid and hold it that way until the contraction passed.

When each pain was over her mother bathed her face with a wet rag and talked softly. She took out a pair of white cotton gloves and slipped them on her daughter's hands to save her from making the blisters worse.

She said, "I've tried to remember my own labor when Ella was born. I remember being in pain but nothing like she is going through. Missy, are you sure that this is going the way it should? I feel certain that if it had been this hard, I'd have remembered it. But then, I was at home in my own bed with a doctor close by and my husband sitting downstairs with our families. My mother sat at my bedside, holding my hand when the pains got bad. She said I squeezed her fingers and even though it hurt, she thought it helped. You want to squeeze my fingers, Ella? Here, hold my hands, maybe it will give you something to push against. I do want to make it easier for you if I can. Anyway, Doctor Hayes spent most of his time downstairs drinking coffee and smoking cigars. I think my mother and my husband's sister, Catherine, did most of the actual tending until the very end when Ella was being born."

She nodded to Ella and continued, "Then the doctor showed up and caught you in a blanket and acted as though he had done something spectacular. You were such a pretty little thing. I remember thinking that you looked so much like your papa. They got us both all cleaned up and you nursed for a few minutes and then they called everyone up to show us off. It was like a party. I was tired, but I was so happy and proud. Your papa and the doctor lit up their big stinky cigars and my mama shooed them out of the room so that we could rest. It was such a happy day. I do wish that we were there now and all of the family was together. It wasn't meant to be this way, Ella; having a baby is supposed to be a happy time."

Mrs. Bledsoe got up from kneeling at her daughter's side and walked downstairs to the back door for a breath of air. She threw the pan of warm dirty water out into the yard and used the gourd dipper to fill it with fresh cool water from the bucket of well water that Joe put there on the little porch every morning. Ella's room was so hot and stuffy that she could barely stand it, but Missy insisted that the windows had to be closed to prevent the bad air from coming in. She said a chill could make both the mother and the baby sick. There was no chance of anyone catching a chill in the kind of heat wave they were having lately. It was hot and sticky. A breeze of any kind would be welcome in there. She'd be more worried about a heat stroke than anyone catching a chill.

Rita Bledsoe's stiff black dress was soaked with sweat. Her long gray-streaked black hair had come unpinned and she ran her fingers through it and let what little breeze there was pass through to cool her scalp. Then she twisted it back into a tight little bun at the nape of her neck and fastened it with the pins her older sister had given her many years ago for a birthday gift. Seeing those pins made her more homesick than usual. She was convinced that after this child was born, she and Ella would find a way to get back to Pennsylvania and rejoin life as it should be. She'd make up a story to explain her daughter's lack of a husband. None of it mattered anymore. She simply had to get out of Alabama and back to her own kind or she'd go crazy or die and she wasn't ready to give in to either fate. She went to her sitting room and retrieved a thick paper fan, thinking that Ella surely would not get a chill from that. Fanning her daughter would give her something constructive to do. She felt helpless and useless and a bit of fanning might help them both.

Another contraction began and Missy tried once more to get her patient to breathe in short puffs but Ella could not seem to concentrate on anything except screaming. When it was over, she begged for a drink of water but Missy told her again that eating or drinking would make her sick to her stomach. She kept on saying for her to think of something else, but that wasn't easy to do when her body felt as though it was being torn in half. Missy told her that she had a good-sized baby in there and he was going to have to come out one way or another. Ella just wanted it to be over.

"Missy, can't you cut open my belly and take the baby out? I overheard Papa and Mr. Whittington say they'd done that once for a cow. They said Papa had read about it in one of his farm books. He used a big sewing needle and horse hair to stitch up the cow's side and both the cow and the calf had lived. It couldn't hurt a bit more than going on like I am. I can't take much more of this. Please do something."

Missy said, "Chile, you ain't no cow and I wouldn't have no idea of how to do that kind of thing even if you was. I ain't goin' to cut anybody's belly open. That is the scariest thing I ever heard of. Maybe a doctor would know how to do sumpin' like that but I sure don't. Now you lay back there and take a deep breath and try to relax like I told you. We gone have to get this done the onliest way we know how."

Chapter Four

When that pain was finished, Ella lay back to think and wait for the next wave of pain that would be coming all too soon.

She wished that none of it was happening. It had all been a mistake from the very beginning. What she had done was wrong. It hadn't seemed so wrong at the time, but now she was sorry for all of it. She wanted to go back in time and do everything differently, beginning with Raymond.

She wished she'd never even seen Raymond, the handsome Negro stable hand who had worked on the farm last fall. She didn't even know his last name. She probably should have asked him. It didn't seem important at the time. Even if they were not married, it would have been good to know the family name so she could tell his child one day. Nobody ever seemed to think of the coloreds as having last names other than the name of the plantation owners who had owned them as slaves. It might not seem right anymore, with the great Emancipation, but it was just the way things were.

Raymond was good with horses. Her father mentioned it at dinner one night. He'd found the young man working for next to nothing at the livery stable in town and made him a job offer on the spot. The next morning when Ella went to the stables, he was there caring for her horse, Maggie, and he casually offered her a hand to help her get into the saddle. As the days passed, the young man grew bolder and would offer his hands for her foot if they were away from the mounting block. He put his hands on her waist to help her down from the saddle another time. She didn't actually need his help or his touching but she didn't try to stop him from doing it. She knew that she should have, but he'd smiled at her. He smiled a lot. The first time he touched her hand in a way that had nothing to do with being helpful, she was so shocked that she didn't say anything. She tried to pretend that it had been an accident or that it had never happened. Evidently, he took that as approval and touched her shoulder the next time she came to the stables to ride Maggie. He hadn't done or said anything rude or suggestive; in fact, he simply reached out in conversation the way anyone would. It was just too familiar somehow. But she thought about it later in her own room and admitted to herself that she didn't mind.

It was unusual for a colored man to be so bold with a white girl. He smiled often and looked her in the eye rather than down at the ground like most of the local black men would have done. She took it as flirting and was annoyed at first and she very nearly told her mother about his impertinence. The problem was that he was one of the few people around the farm that bothered to talk to her at all and after a while, she began to like the attention. He was a tall good-looking young man with smooth unblemished skin the color of coffee-milk. He was a smooth talker so it didn't take very long for the two of them to form a friendship. His youth and enthusiasm gave him confidence and made him believe that they could be friends and the color of their skin had nothing to do with it. It wasn't so much that he'd taken advantage as that they simply enjoyed being together. They talked about anything that popped into their minds, and Ella had never had such an open friendship before. She thoroughly enjoyed their conversations whatever the topic. He made her laugh, and laughter was a rare commodity in her life. She wanted to believe such a relationship was possible.

Her own father, being a Quaker, had believed in the equality of the races and had passed those beliefs on to his daughter. He'd treated every worker on the plantation as if they were his equal in the sight of God. Her mother did not share her husband's liberal beliefs, however, and told Ella that she should not be so familiar with the servants and the workers. She often reminded Ella that she was far above them in station and she must be personable but not to get personal.

It was a confusing situation and she never felt certain which people were equal and which were not. It seemed simpler to believe like her father and try to be polite and kind to everyone.

Eventually, both she and Raymond grew bolder, and their friendship grew into something more physical. Over the few months they were friends, they shared books, held hands, and eventually kissed. She enjoyed the attention and found everything about the experience to be exciting. She woke up thinking of him and went to sleep with him on her mind. They met whenever Raymond had the time and were very careful not to be seen together. She tried to believe their being together was right but she knew the personal things they did together were morally wrong according to her upbringing. The two of them never discussed religion, so she didn't know if he was a Christian or not. It didn't matter anymore. He'd never know he had become a father.

The last afternoon they spent together was as fresh in her mind as if it were yesterday. It was early February and the weather was unseasonably warm. It looked as though there wasn't going to be a winter at all that year. The sun was bright and the flowers and fruit trees were in early bloom. She'd taken Maggie out for a very short run and came back specifically to be with Raymond. She found him cleaning a horse stall and had sneaked up behind him. On a mad whim, she traced the beads of sweat with her finger as they dripped down the middle of his back. She thought he was beautiful and couldn't help wanting to touch him.

He laughed and told her, "You ort to not do that, Miss Ella. It's gone be likely to get you into trouble."

She said, "I don't want any trouble, Raymond, but I liked it when you kissed me before. I want you to do it again."

He said, "Well, if you mean that, girl, then I'd be happy to oblige. Today's been one a dem days when I got ma chores done early and dere's no better way to spend a little time than sharing kisses wid a pretty girl. Dat's for sure."

He'd then gone to the water bucket and pulled out a rag to wash up a bit. Ella stood there watching and marveling at his strong arms and flat belly. They'd snuggled down into the hay kissing and discovering each other and finally made love. Ella had been swept into the lovemaking but went willingly and never once thought of stopping. Afterwards, they lay there touching and talking for a long time. She enjoyed putting her pale hands on his darker skin and looking at the contrast. Raymond said it was like coffee and cream. She couldn't understand how some whites thought colored people like him were not human. He was as human as she was and as perfectly made as anyone she'd ever laid eyes on. He had a quick mind and a sense of humor that kept her remembering his little stories and jokes all day long.

Just as they'd begun to put their clothes back on, there had been one brief moment when they both grew afraid of being caught. Joe and Missy's twelve-year-old nephew Sammy came into the barn to get some food for Joe's mule. He might have heard them moving around in the hay pile because they saw him stop and listen as they peeked at him through the wide slats that helped keep the hay from scattering. They froze and didn't even take a breath. Sammy must have been in a hurry because he quickly put a scoop of food in his bucket and ran out of the barn to finish his chores.

Ella fell back in the hay, covered her face with her hands, and giggled. Her heart was pounding from the fear and pure excitement of the moment. Raymond relaxed a little but she could tell that his heart was pounding just as much as hers. He knew, even more than she, that their getting caught together in a haystack would not go well for him. He jumped up as soon as the coast was clear and began picking up the hay they'd scattered.

Ella put her clothes to rights and began to chatter. She asked him if he intended to stay here or did he have plans for the rest of his life? She told him that she wanted to do something useful in the future but didn't know what that might be. She hoped that her life would be different after she and her mother went back up to Philadelphia to live with her grandparents.

He'd said, "I want to be like a rolling stone. I want to go travelin' and see what the rest of this big ole country looks like. I got me a map and I think I'm gone head up north for a spell and then I want to go out west and maybe even try myself at being a cowboy. I'm gone save my money and get me a big ole hat and some of them leather pants, they call chaps."

He was fascinated by the idea of following the huge herds of cattle to market. He said the cowboys slept under the stars and he liked working with the animals. Ella read several of the dime novels that he'd bought. The stories made being a cowboy sound like the most exciting job a young man could hope to find. He told her all about his dreams. Ella was entranced and wished that she had that kind of freedom for herself.

She didn't want to be a cowboy, but she certainly understood his restlessness. She didn't have any dreams of her own, but Raymond had enough to share, and she enjoyed listening to him. He was the happiest and most carefree person that she'd ever met in her entire life. There were times when she wished there were some way for her to run away with him. He was going on a great adventure and she was stuck in Alabama with little to occupy her mind or her hands. They spent most of the middle of the day together. For the first time in her life, Ella had a friend and she was enjoying every minute of it.

The next day when she went out to ride, there was a new stable hand who told her that he didn't know where the other man had gone. She did not show her disappointment but she missed Raymond's company and his smile.

She missed doing the things they had shared together in spite of the nagging fear that those things were probably the biggest sins she had ever committed in her life. She wondered if she had scared him away or said the wrong thing to him and hurt his feelings somehow. She cried herself to sleep that night and then decided to accept what they'd shared as a gift. It had been joyful and sweet and at least she would have those memories to carry with her no matter how lonely her life might be in the future.

Raymond would never know he had become a father. The truth was that his knowing wouldn't have made it any easier anyway. It was probably better that he never knew. During their brief time together, he'd been kind to her and they had enjoyed good times. Deep inside her heart, Ella knew that there had never been any chance of them sharing anything but pleasure and daydreams. Even with the Emancipation, some relationships were not accepted in rural Alabama and might never be. If he had stayed around, the chances were great that someone would have discovered their secret and then Raymond would have been the one blamed for it, no matter how much she protested or supported him. There had been other relationships like theirs and from what she'd heard whispered among the workers, they usually ended up badly. There were horrible stories of hangings and murder, so it was best that he left when he did. Her own reputation in the family and around town was about to be ruined. There was no reason that both of them should suffer from the mistakes they'd made. It was probably best for all concerned. But it still hurt.

Chapter Five

It wasn't long after Raymond's departure that her father died suddenly. The plantation was thrown into turmoil once again. First, the war had stopped the farming completely for several years and then just as things were building up again, a horrible fire the previous summer had severely damaged the house and destroyed the big barn. Several of the local workmen, including one of Slimmy's brothers, had died trying to rescue the mules and horses. Mrs. Whittington was seriously burned when her skirt caught on fire and was still in Natchez being cared for by her daughter. Mr. Whittington and Mr. Bledsoe had been trying their best to put things back together at the plantation but Mr. Whittington's heart was no longer in it. It was a struggle for them all. The rumors buzzing through the black community said that they might just close down the whole plantation and sell off the land. Some of the workers were scared that they'd no longer have jobs, and for the second time in their lives, they were worried about how they'd feed their families. Mr. Bledsoe's death would likely have some effect on all of them.

Ella and her mother got caught up in grief for several weeks. After the funeral, they began to make plans to return to Pennsylvania with intentions of leaving as soon as they settled their business dealings and sold the house. Mrs. Bledsoe tried to sell it back to the Whittingtons but they were having problems of their own and did not want the place. Since the land was surrounded by Whittington Plantation, there wasn't much chance of selling it to anyone who had hopes of expansion, and none of the local farmers or the plantation owners had the funds to buy a farm because of their own losses during the war. Most of them were struggling to build up the land they had and didn't want to take on any more.

Ella and her mother stayed in bed until late in the mornings because they missed Mr. Bledsoe and because they no longer had a reason to get up early. It was a sad and frustrating time for them all. Ella began to feel sick and stayed in her bed even more. She thought it was just the sadness from her father's passing until they discovered her condition.

Missy came to her room one morning to ask if she had any rags from her monthlies that needed washing. Ella didn't and suddenly realized that it had been nearly four months since her regular cycle of bleeding. She had been caught up in the misery of learning to live without seeing Raymond, and then her father died. Missy was surprised but Ella didn't know what to think. Missy sat her down and gently asked her about things she might have done with a boy and Ella confessed that she had done those things but didn't tell her the boy's name. Missy was astounded but tried hard not to show it. Ella was surprised to learn that what she and Raymond did had caused a baby to grow inside her. She'd had no idea that she could get caught that way. She kept saying over and over, "But Missy, I'm not married. How can I be having a baby?"

Missy patted her hand and told her, "Chile, not having a piece of paper saying you are married ain't what caused this. What you did with that boy on the river bank or in the haystack is what did it. I seen lots of girls get that way because of a sweet-talkin' man. You ain't the onliest one, fer sure. But first we gone hafta figger out a way to tell your mama about this latest development and I promise you, she ain't gone be happy about it. You know she done made arrangements for y'all to be headin' back up north to live with your relatives. This little sit-i-ation of yours is gone knock a big hole in her plans. Oh Lawdy! Come on, Miss Ella, let's get it over with. I don' know what's gone happen, but I do know the sooner we tell her, the sooner she's gone have her say and then maybe give us all some peace."

Her mother was just as outraged as they'd expected. It was a perfect example of what Slimmy called "a hissy-fit." She yelled, clutched her bible to her chest, and told Ella how disappointed she was to have a daughter who behaved like common trash. She stormed around in a huff for days. Ella didn't argue with her or talk back a single time. There really wasn't much she could say to defend herself. She knew that she had done something that was going to change their lives forever.

Finally, her mother wrote to the family and told them that Ella had an illness and they would have to wait until the fever passed and she had recovered her strength. The relatives in Pennsylvania believed that south Alabama was a place of fevers and sickness anyway, so they would easily accept the lies. Ella was already over a third of the way through the pregnancy when they found out about it, so there was nothing to do but wait until after the baby was born. There would be no snow for either of them at Christmas that year.

Ella moaned and asked again, "Dear lord, when will the pain go away? Please make it get over soon. I don't want to feel pain like this ever again. I've learned my lesson, I swear I have. I'll never do it again," she prayed aloud.

Missy had told her earlier in the day that her own mother had had eleven children. There was no way Ella wanted to go through the experience of birth ten more times. She couldn't imagine anyone going through it half that many times. No wonder Missy's poor little mama had looked so old and shriveled up before she died. She was worn out from having and raising eleven children. Now Ella understood being an only child herself and didn't blame her mother one bit.

Chapter Six

Rita Grayson Bledsoe had once been a dark-haired beauty with laughing blue eyes and a pleasant voice. She was tall, slim, and fond of pretty dresses and parasols. Her father was a judge and her mother was a pampered lady. She'd had several young men seek her company, but was thrilled when the banker's son began to call on her. He was a handsome, well-educated man and considered to be quite the catch by all her friends. She felt proud to walk with him in public and to see the looks they received when they were together. It was said they made a striking couple. Their wedding had been a grand event with half the town showing up to wish them well. Their lives were laid out in perfect fashion and Rita became a happily married young lady with a beautiful home and a husband that she adored. A year later she was blessed with a precious daughter and thought her life was complete and couldn't get any better.

Everyone expected John Bledsoe to stay in the family banking business, so they were all shocked and dismayed when, six years later, he announced his own personal dream and his plans to make it come true. He'd always been interested in farming and wanted to go into farm management to help in the reconstruction of the South after the Civil War. Rita knew that men talked about new ideas and social experiments, but no one she'd ever known had actually followed those paths. She thought those topics were just things men talked about after dinner with their brandy and cigars. She'd openly admired his lofty ideas, but certainly never thought he'd try to follow through with them. His own father tried to talk him into opening a southern bank, if he wanted to be helpful, but John Bledsoe had decided that he was meant for a higher calling. He wanted to devote his life to Social Justice. Rita decided to think of it as a noble gesture. Her husband was trying to make that ravaged part of the world a better place. She swallowed the hard knot of fear and put on a brave face, trying to look at the upcoming trip to Alabama as a big adventure. John was a banker. Physical labor was very different from sitting at a desk. She secretly hoped that her husband would come to his senses after a few weeks of hard work put blisters on his hands.

Mr. Bledsoe had never been to rural Alabama but he was confident that it wouldn't be very different from rural Pennsylvania. A farm was still a farm, after all.

He convinced his young wife that they would have a simpler life but it would be filled with the satisfaction of knowing they were doing something worthwhile. They wouldn't be alone. He hoped she would quickly make new friends among the other farm managers' wives and families. She could give dinner parties and have ladies over for tea just as she did in Pennsylvania. He told her that she could even start a reading group.

She was a strong woman and would make the best of it as any lady would. Her grandparents had a farm and she'd always enjoyed visiting there as a child. There would be servants to do the work and he believed her life would probably not change too much. She would stay in touch with her friends and relatives by writing lots of letters. He convinced her that her sisters would come to visit her and she would be able to visit with them as often as she liked. And so she climbed onto the passenger train the day they left determined to be the best farm manager's wife that she could be.

The trip was long and difficult. John had been so caught up in his own big dream that he could not see that Rita was frightened. The countryside that passed the windows of the train was bleak and ravaged by war. There were few towns and no cities to get her excited. She was even more dismayed when they arrived at the station in rural Alabama. She got a hint of how different their lives would actually be. No one met them at the station. There were no maids or footmen to help with the luggage. They had to hire an open wagon instead of a carriage and then pay someone familiar with the area to drive them out to their house, which was miles out in the country.

The choking red dust flew up behind the wagon wheels and covered the weeds that grew beside the road and settled on their cases in the back of the wagon. The heat and humidity were stifling. There were dark faces everywhere. Rita had never been around many Negroes and found herself very uncomfortable in their company. It was nothing like she had imagined it to be.

Thank goodness, the house had been aired and was relatively clean, but it was much smaller and less attractive than she expected. There were only Missy, Joe, and Slimmy to help with the move and the upkeep of the house. All three of them looked middle aged and scared as John gave them orders to unload their belongings.

Rita had been mortified and very glad her family could not see how low she'd landed on the social ladder. She was determined not to let her disappointment show. She sat down to write to her sisters and her friends as soon as they were unpacked and settled in. She made her situation sound much more elegant than it really was. She figured that a little exaggeration was better than complaining. After a few more days, she began to wish she could ask her father to come get her, but knew that she wouldn't because her parents would expect her to be supportive of her husband. She was not one to give up and would find a way to endure whatever came her way. That was what good wives did. She was determined that her tears would be shed in the privacy of her own room and no one would see her unhappiness.

Mr. Bledsoe was following his own dreams and had given up the idea of social status completely. Rather than being popular, he was more interested in social experiments and implementing new farming techniques that he hoped would make the land produce more than it had before the war. He read up on animal husbandry and became quite familiar with the different kinds of hogs that were grown by the local farms. He and Mr. Whittington tried new strains of seeds and even planted sugar cane and peanuts to see if they would be easier to grow than cotton.

Somehow with all the loneliness and lack of social contact, Rita lost her sweet smile and over the years turned into a bitter and prudish woman who tried to impose her own rigid moral code on her daughter and everyone else around her. The changes were slow but drastic. Mr. Bledsoe hardly recognized the woman she became.

Ella remembered her mother laughing and singing when she was a little girl up north. But even then Ella had spent most of her time with the servants while her mother visited with her friends and relatives. There was a pretty young governess from Ireland who taught her to draw and allowed her to eat sugar on her bread at tea. The housekeepers were busy with daily chores but watched after the girl. They allowed her a lot of freedom as long as she wasn't doing anything to get dirty or hurt herself. It had been a pleasant enough way to live and she often had her cousins to play games with and to keep her company. She barely remembered their faces and would not recognize any of them if they came to the door.

In Alabama, Missy and Slimmy took care of her, but there were no playmates and few toys. There was no nursery or governess. There were no cousins who loved to sing or play games. She'd enjoyed following Missy to the garden to pick vegetables to cook for their meals and watching Joe mend a fence or build a shed. Slimmy even let her stand on a wooden box and wash the dishes until her mother caught her and let everyone know that her child was not going to help them with their chores. Slimmy had been quite put out by that. She liked having the help and felt every young girl should know how to wash dishes. Rita Bledsoe disagreed.

Rita spent her long and lonely days writing overly cheerful letters to her family up north and studying the Bible. She interpreted the Scriptures in her own way. She'd never quite grasped her husband's Quaker ideas but had been willing to try when they lived with his Quaker family. They were kind people who showed her tolerance and did their best to teach her that soft words made life more pleasant. After seeing so much on the plantation that went against her own upbringing and watching her husband struggle to turn things around and make the farm into the kind of place he believed it could be, she began to change her mind and miss the righteous anger of her old religion. She missed the fire and brimstone preachers of her youth and tried to remember what they had said. She began to see her loss of social standing as a punishment for some unnamed sin, and began to see God as a strict disciplinarian instead of the loving God that she had worshiped in the recent past. She became a Bible-pounding religious fanatic married to a soft-spoken Quaker man. with no ministers or friends of either religion available to offer guidance. She taught Ella to read and write by making her study the Scriptures and taught her to count the verses. Ella learned her lessons well enough. She did not accept her mother's religious fervor, but gave lip-service to avoid the loud verbal abuse her mother would heap upon her if she said something that went against her rigid moral code. Rita believed the Bible to be literally the word of God and found plenty there to tell her exactly how God felt about pretty much everything that Ella or anyone else did, or at least her own interpretation of it.

If she asked questions, her father would tell her about his own beliefs during the rare times when they went out riding together, and she took bits of truth from one parent and then from the other, becoming thoroughly confused by both.

When his wife would go off on one of her religious tirades, Mr. Bledsoe would think up a reason to be excused and go to the barn or the fields, anything to find something else to do until she calmed down. He eventually retreated into his own private world of books and charts and reading about the European social experiments. After a while the family structure broke down completely. They were three separate people sharing a space with little contact with each other. The years passed slowly for Ella and her mother. Mrs. Bledsoe continued to dream of the day when they would visit the relatives in Pennsylvania and rejoin the social circles that she missed so desperately. After her husband died, she was free to go home and could think of nothing else until she found out about her daughter's pregnancy.

Rita Bledsoe became so angry and frustrated that she began telling her daughter that God would punish her for her sins by giving her pain and suffering. The young and impressionable girl believed it completely and accepted that she was going to suffer. During labor, she pushed as hard as she could to rid herself of the guilt as well as to get the birth over as fast as possible.

Chapter Seven

Ella began to moan and writhe in agony again. She begged Missy to do something to stop the pains. They were coming closer together and she was weakening.

Even though she'd seen many girls in labor, Missy was feeling sorry for the agony this girl was going through. Missy didn't believe that God would use pain and suffering to punish a young woman for her mistakes. She'd see some who would have deserved pain and suffering but sailed through the birth as though it was nothing worse than monthly cramps. She knew that Ella was an innocent. She wished there was a way to help her get through the ordeal. She didn't have much in her birthing kit to slow the labor or dull the pain. There were herbs that her mama had used but Missy couldn't always find where they grew and she wasn't nearly as sure of how to recognize or prepare them, or what their effects were as her mama had been. Missy depended more on prayers to get through the birthing than herbs and tonics, but watching Ella suffer had finally gotten to her enough that she dug in her bag for the small cloth sacks containing the little medicine she did carry with her. She headed off to the kitchen and poured boiling water over a handful of shredded willow bark in a cup to make a tea for the pain and offered her patient a couple of large sips of the bitter liquid as soon as it was cool enough to drink. After an hour, she still couldn't tell that it was doing much to help. She gave the girl another big spoonful of the bitter tea and prayed for Jesus to take away the pain. The willow bark tea might help a little, but her mother had warned her to use it sparingly because it was also said to cause more bleeding. Folk medicine to Missy was almost a guessing game with so many things to remember, and she had to hope that things would go well for the girl.

She'd gone over everything in her mind and could think of nothing else to do. The baby might be stuck somehow and as far as she could remember there was nothing left to do but watch and pray and wish that her own mama was there to show her what to do. When it was closer to the time for the baby to be born then maybe she could try to turn the baby if it was still hung up or turned wrong, but for the moment there was nothing she could do.

At times like this, she wished that she had taken the time to write down all of the things she needed to know in a notebook so that she would have it to look at whenever she had questions. Her mother never learned to read or write, but Missy could have taken notes. She'd never realized that she might have a hard time remembering things after her mother was gone.

Ella interrupted her thoughts by crying out from the ongoing contraction. Her screams had finally become less frequent but not because the pain was any less. The girl was so exhausted that she lay there moaning and holding onto the metal bed frame for support as she pushed until the peak of each contraction. Her mother once again shoved the padded stick into her mouth to give her something to bite down on. She had bitten the stick so much that her lips were bruised and her gums were leaving bloody marks on the cloth wrapping.

Rita Bledsoe was worried. She had not been exposed to many birthing situations, but the knot of nervousness in her insides told her that things were not going well. She thought maybe she should have sent for the doctor. They were moving away in a few weeks, so perhaps it wouldn't have mattered whether anyone found out about the baby. The people in town didn't know any of her family up north anyway. If things didn't improve very soon, she would send Joe to get the doctor. It would take less than an hour to get him to the house.

Missy wiped her own sweaty face with a flour sack towel and told the girl, "You got to stop that screamin', Miss Ella. It ain't helpin'anybody. That hollering is taking away the strength that you orta be putting into pushin'. All that yellin' is gone do is give you a real bad sore throat. It sure ain't helping the baby to come out and it is giving me a headache something fierce." She took a swallow of the willow bark tea straight from the cup to stop her own pain. She noticed her hands were shaking as she set the cup back on the table.

It was time for this thing to get over and she was tired and worried and her head was pounding. She decided to check on the baby and then go out to the kitchen and pour herself another cup of coffee. It would be scorched by now from sitting on the stove so long but she didn't care. She hoped there was a cold biscuit left to go along with it. She needed the energy and she needed a break.

Ella closed her eyes and mumbled about being sorry about screaming. She was very tired. She knew she couldn't stand much more of the pain and had little strength left for pushing, and her throat was already sore. She was hurting in so many places that the sore throat was only noticeable when she tried to talk. Her voice was husky and scratchy when she begged Missy to make the pain stop.

Missy placed her hand on top of the girl's swollen belly, waited for the next contraction to get going, and then pushed down as the contraction took hold, trying to help the baby come out faster. She pushed harder until Ella began to holler and moan again. Then as she moved down to check the progress, she saw it coming. The infant's head was pushing against the skin and stretching the opening.

She said, "Thank you, Lord Jesus. Here it comes, Miss Ella. I can see the top of yor baby's head. One more good push ought to do it. You jes' let yo'self get loose and go with the pain. You breathe like I told you. Let your body tell you when to push and then you give it all you got. I will try to help by pushing up here. Here we go, let's get this young'un born and we'll get to see if it is a boy or a girl. It's been a long hard day, but it is almost over." She reached a small wooden spoon into her pot of lard, got a big glob and rubbed it on her hands to make them slippery so she could ease them around the baby's head and help it slip out of its mama's body and into the world that was waiting for it.

Missy stared at the purple-tinted infant, whose dark curly head was being pushed from this white girl's body, with fear and a touch of something else that wasn't easily defined. Surprise, pity, remorse, sadness, there were too many confusing emotions even to bother to try to put into words. Miss Ella wasn't the first white girl in south Alabama to give birth to a dark-skinned baby for sure and she probably wouldn't be the last, but Missy was afraid. She ran her hands down her bloodstained apron and bent over to catch the infant in a clean flour sack towel as he emerged. She did have to wonder who fathered the babe. There weren't many men or boys who'd worked for the Bledsoes. It had to be one of the transient workers who'd passed through last year. If Miss Ella had been messing around with one of the local boys, Missy would've heard about it. There could be big trouble coming from this for sure. She was glad that Mr. Bledsoe was gone to heaven. Some kind of nagging primitive instinct told her that this day would bring her misery for a very long time and she was not going to be able to stop it, no matter how hard she tried.

The tired muscles in Ella's belly squeezed, pushed, and forced the wiggling bundle of humanity out of his warm growing place and into the folded-up towels in Missy's waiting hands. He was a healthy baby and Missy had been forced to grease the girl's woman parts with hog lard and still had to reach inside and tug at him and finally turn him over to get him delivered. He'd been trying to come out face up and that had been part of the problem. Now he was born and she had to admit that he was a fine baby boy, strong and well made. She laid him down on Ella's soft belly and tied the cord with cotton string in two places and cut between them with her knife. He opened his dark eyes and blinked a time or two, took his first breath of air, and cried almost as loudly as his mother had. Ella smiled weakly and closed her eyes. She was so tired that she didn't even have the strength to hold her child. "In a minute, my sweet baby," she said, "let me catch my breath and rest here for just a minute."

"Go ahead and cry, baby boy, you prob'ly goin' to have a lot to cry about a'for dis is done," Missy said to him softly as she wiped the birthing fluids from his wrinkled little face and squirming body and wrapped him securely in one of the clean blankets stacked neatly beside her. She then placed him on his belly in the bureau drawer that had been prepared for his arrival. He hunched up on his knees with his little rump in the air, pushed one hand up to his mouth, and sucked on it hungrily. Missy hoped that little fist would hold him until they got Miss Ella cleaned up and ready to give him the nourishment that he needed. He was a fine baby and was going to need his mother's milk as soon as possible.

Chapter Eight

Missy thought, *No hand-made cradle would hold this baby. No lovin' arms or soft words would make him feel welcome on the day of his birth. But all the same, he was a big healthy baby boy with sturdy arms and legs and a good strong cry.* She was pleased and hoped that his life would not be too hard.

Her own mama used to tell her and her brothers and sisters that what don't kill you would make you stronger. Missy hoped this child would be strong enough to weather the storms ahead, because he was bound to have more than a few to get through. Mixed-blood children had to be strong to survive, especially in the white man's world this one was born into. His mama would face her share of emotional turmoil over it too. That young girl had no idea of what she was going to have to face while trying to raise this child. It was going to take a lot of courage and strength for sure. She even wondered if it might not be better to ask Miss Ella if she wanted to give him up to be raised by a local Negro family. It would probably make her mother happier. They could leave for that place up north and get on with their lives without having to explain a racially mixed baby. It might go easier for the boy as well. A lot of Negro families had light-colored babies from the days of slavery and everyone accepted them and got on with their lives.

Rita was talking softly to her daughter and offering comforting words, but showed no interest in the baby. She'd already said that he was not a Bledsoe and would never be one. That came as no surprise to Missy. The woman's shock and instant hatred were written all over her face as soon as she saw the child. She wiped her daughter's face with a damp cloth and told her that it was almost over. Ella leaned back against the quilts and pillows and closed her eyes again. Missy was glad that the screaming had stopped but was concerned that Ella was less responsive. Usually by now, a first-time mama was anxious to see her child, to hold him and count his fingers and toes. They wanted to take the baby to breast and smile and brag about how handsome he was or guess which side of the family he looked like. A short break was all right, but it was time now for the afterbirth to come and for Ella to regain some of her strength and enthusiasm.

Missy began to rub the girl's belly and talk to her. "Come on now, Miss Ella, we got us one more job to do and then we can get you cleaned up and let you hold your baby. He is a fine little man. Now, let's get the afterbirth delivered and then we can get you cleaned up and make you more comfortable."

Missy knew it was important that the body rid itself of the afterbirth and then the new mama could get on with feeding her baby. There was some kind of a connection between pushing out the afterbirth and the starting up of milk production. She didn't know exactly how it worked, but her mama said it was really important. Another important thing was that the afterbirth had to come out because it could cause a fever if it stayed inside the mother. She rubbed Ella's flaccid belly and tried to make the muscles tighten up again. There should be some contractions almost like birth pains, though not quite the same and usually not as hard. Instead, the girl's belly lay there soft and flabby from being stretched over the last few months. Missy tugged at the cord a little to try to pull it out but was afraid that she might break it off and that could be bad too. When it didn't come, Missy continued to massage the soft stomach as hard as she could and prayed for it to tighten up.

Rita Bledsoe had been shocked and dismayed when she saw the dark-skinned infant being born. When the baby appeared, instead of being red, bald, and wrinkled, he was tan and dusky colored with a head full of kinky dark hair and full features.

She'd been trying to figure out exactly who'd caused this thing ever since they found out that Ella was carrying. The only men around here were the workers. She thought, *Surely, Ella had not been messing around with a Negro worker! I taught my daughter better than that. Was it possible that she'd been raped? Wouldn't she have said something? Ella is an independent sort of girl but she'd never behaved in any way that would have led me to believe that she was seeing a man. She spent most of her free time in the stables with her horse, Maggie. She was naïve in many ways and had no knowledge of the actions of men and women. She'd never been told about sex or romance. Her father had also shielded her from anything having to do with the animals breeding on the farm, so it was simply not possible that she had known anything at all about what went on between males and females of any species. I'm sure of it.*

She remembered one incident in particular that her husband told her about one night. Ella rode her horse down to the hog pens to ask her father if they could go to town the next day. The men were all gathered around the pen watching a boar take a sow and were laughing and being coarse and rowdy as men sometimes did when they were watching animals in such situations. Her husband had not expected to see Ella riding up and went to great lengths to steer her away from the area so that she would not witness the mating of the hogs. Ella asked what was happening and her father said that there was a little situation with the pigs, but that the workers had it under control and she seemed to have accepted his word and never questioned either of them about it. Mr. Bledsoe only mentioned it so that Rita could be prepared to give her some kind of answer if Ella asked. She never brought up the subject at all.

I never saw the girl behave in a flirtatious manner or try to draw attention to herself either. In fact, she'd been painfully shy and kept to the background whenever strangers were around. Who could have done this thing? There is one sure thing. If I find out who the culprit is, I'll see to it that he's hung from the nearest tree. Somebody is going to pay for this atrocity.

The new complication was going to ruin all her plans for going home to Pennsylvania. She wondered why young people only thought of themselves. She felt young people were selfish. God must surely look down and be disappointed in all of them. The world He had created truly was a wicked place and especially this part of it. She desperately wanted to go back to Pennsylvania and the recent complication was something she needed to think about for a while. Something would have to be done, that's all. She'd find a way.

She thought to herself, *Perhaps I could manage to get Missy to take that baby away and give it to a family of his own kind. I think I could convince Eloise that the baby was born dead or that it died right after he was born and then after she had a few months to heal, we could go on to Pennsylvania as though nothing had happened at all. Perhaps there is a way to salvage the situation. It is a good plan. I'll mention it to Missy as soon as we get Ella cleaned up. It's really the only solution that makes any sense. Surely Missy will see that. She will have to find the child a home. He is her kind. It would certainly be better for the child as well. Anyone with any sense at all would know that.*

Rita wondered what Missy was waiting for. She was fussing and wiping and muttering to herself and mashing around on Ella's belly and saying something about the afterbirth needing to come out. Evidently, it was taking longer than Missy wanted it to.

"Oh God, don't tell me there could be another one in there," Rita prayed out loud.

"No Ma'am, there ain't another baby. I am jes' trying to get the afterbirth to come out. It's s'posed to come on its own, but it looks like I am gone have to reach inside and pull it out by hand if it don't hurry up. I don't like to have to do that. It can make things harder on the mama and it can cause childbed fever."

She'd heard about times when other midwives put their hands inside the mother's body and the mother died of fever several days after the baby was born. Her mama had told her that it was caused by dirty hands and Missy always kept everything clean for her mamas and had never lost one to fever.

Missy gave a final big push on the mushy belly and the placenta came gushing out of the girl's body all at once as a big red glob of tissue with a lot of blood. Missy was glad to see it although there did seem to be more blood than usual. She gathered the mess up in a towel and set it aside so they could finish cleaning up Miss Ella and get her ready to nurse her new son. She would burn the towel and the afterbirth as part of her cleaning-up ritual. The placenta was not needed after the birth, and the disposal of it was wrapped in secrecy and superstition. Some midwives said it was to be buried, but Missy felt that it was better to burn it as an offering to give thanks to God for the safe delivery. Burning it seemed to be ritual enough for her.

Ella mumbled that she was feeling cold and began to shiver, so Rita gently wiped her daughter's sweaty brow with a cloth and then pulled a blanket up to her neck trying to warm her even though the room was probably hotter than outside. Ella was glad the pain was over. She'd closed her eyes and finally relaxed. The lower half of her body felt numb in a way, empty and tingling like when a foot went to sleep except that there was a kind of achiness left behind too. She had a strange lightheadedness, almost the same as when she had sneaked a taste of Papa's brandy one time, a little dizzy, but it was nice. All she wanted to do was sleep. She told herself that she would hold her baby after she'd had a little rest. Missy could surely take care of him until she felt stronger. Her eyes closed as she drifted away.

Rita began shaking Ella's hand and patting her cheek. Missy was rubbing Ella's belly with both hands and whispering something to herself about the bleeding. Her hands were shaking and her voice was higher pitched, and she sounded even more worried than before the afterbirth came. It made Rita nervous to watch her behaving so strangely.

Ella didn't care anymore. The fact that the pain was gone was truly a blessing. *Maybe God has forgiven me after all,* she thought to herself. She hoped that was true. She'd taken her punishment, if that was what the pain was all about. She'd paid the price for all her sins and now it was finally over. The tingling numbness was all over her body now. Even her face tingled. There was a warm and gentle peace. That part was very nice. She let her spirit drift and float above the bed and toward the ceiling.

Looking down, Ella saw her mother. She looked worried. She saw Missy working desperately hard to staunch the bleeding that would not stop. She felt strangely separate from the body lying on her bed where Missy knotted up her own shaking fists and kneaded them deeply into her belly. Missy muttered prayers aloud, as she squeezed and massaged and begged the flaccid womb to contract. It should have tightened up immediately after the afterbirth came, to cut off the flow of blood that was collecting in a large puddle on the floor at the end of the bed. She refused to give up but was also very much aware that her efforts were not helping at all.

Missy was becoming more afraid with every second that passed. She felt helpless. She'd seen this happen only once before and she didn't know any way to change the outcome. Her mother had been the midwife that other time and she'd told Missy that sometimes it was God's will and there was nothing that could be done. Missy felt guilty and was afraid that she'd helped to cause the reaction by giving the girl the willow bark tea. She tried to justify it by reminding herself that the young woman had been in so much pain and that it was terrible to watch her suffer. Missy was also afraid of what Mrs. Bledsoe would do to her if she found out. Mrs.

Bledsoe wasn't usually violent, but she was large enough and strong enough to do some harm if she put her mind to it. Missy, with her guilt, felt she had reason to fear the woman's wrath.

The young girl looked pasty-white and her skin was clammy from shock. She was so weak that her head had rolled back on the pillows and her eyes were half open with only the whites showing. Missy grabbed a couple of big sticks of firewood, got Mrs. Bledsoe to help her raise the foot of the bed, and then shoved them into place to hold it elevated. She hoped that would hold some of the blood inside the girl's body instead of letting it run out so easily.

There was no time to make an herb tea or poultice. Her mother had told her that the herb pennyroyal would cause the womb to contract but she didn't have any of that in her kit. She had never needed it before and had always felt strange and guilty about carrying it because it could also be used to cause miscarriages and get rid of babies when the mother didn't want to have them. Missy thought that was a sin and never wanted to be associated with that practice and so she never had used pennyroyal before. At that moment, she wished that she had a bag of it in her kit. She would find the place where it grew after today and have it in her kit for the next time she birthed a baby if it was at all possible, because Ella was dying right in front of their eyes and Missy didn't know how to fix it. She felt helpless and afraid.

Rita Bledsoe looked at the blood and said, "Missy, isn't there something we can do to stop it? Why is this happening? What's the matter? I have heard about that happening before but I never thought it would happen to Eloise. You are supposed to know all about these things. Do something!" She felt panic building up inside her and the anger that she had felt for her daughter was quickly dissolved by the blood flowing freely to the floor.

Missy told her, "It happens sometimes, Mrs. Bledsoe. I don't know why, other than it's God's will so, you jes' keep on praying 'cause right now that's all I know to do."

Missy's mind raced as she pushed down and vigorously massaged on the girl's stomach some more. Instead of tightening up as she'd hoped, it continued to wallow there loosely in her hands and the blood kept pouring out. She'd never seen so much blood pour out of a human body. She wondered if the pushing made it worse. She considered whether to push or not to. If only there was a way to put it back in, she thought. She could catch it in a bucket but then she wouldn't know what to do with it. She felt helpless and afraid because she'd never lost a mother before.

She thanked the Lord for the baby being all right. He must surely need to be nursed, but, bless his heart, he was still gnawing on his little fist and sleeping peacefully in his drawer. He was a good baby.

She thought, *I'll have to find someone to take him in as soon as possible. There must be someone nearby who would nurse an orphaned baby, especially one as good as that one. Maybe that Ledbetter girl down the road would take him. She's still nursing her own baby and she's young and strong enough to handle two youngsters at one time. Her man might appreciate a boy to help out on their little farm one day.*

He's a pretty baby too. In a day or so when he's all filled out, he's gone be a real pretty baby. I know in my heart that Mrs. Bledsoe ain't gone want no colored grandbaby. There was so much shock and ugliness in that woman's face when she saw his color. No, she wouldn't want this baby. But that's all right. I am gone find a home for him. I'm gone find him a mama who will take good care of him. If I cain't find anyone then I'll take him and raise him myself. I'll find a way. He is a fine-looking boy and I want to do what I can to help him. Joe and me can raise him up if we got to. We got a cow. We both getting up there in age and a strong healthy boy would be a big help to us a few years from now. Joe can teach him to hunt and fish and farm.

But first, she had to try again to stop his mama's bleeding. She pressed down on the girl's belly as hard as she could and held her hands there until her arms were shaking. Missy knew there was nothing she could do to stop it, but she had to keep trying. She was having a hard time with it emotionally as well as physically. She couldn't give up. She had to keep working at it.

So far nothing had worked and her prayers were not being answered the way that she'd hoped. She'd asked that God's will be done and hoped that His will was the same as her own. Evidently His will was for Ella to pass on.

Mrs. Bledsoe was going to take it hard, for sure. Missy felt sorry for her. Some things were so sad that no explanation was enough. She decided to continue to work as hard as she could so that Mrs. Bledsoe couldn't say that she had stopped trying too soon. It was all going to be over in a few more minutes and at least she would know that she had done her best to save the girl and Mrs. Bledsoe would know it too.

Chapter Nine

Ella watched it all with only fleeting interest as she floated past the ceiling and followed the soft glowing light inside the tunnel that appeared before her. She wished that she could tell Missy and her mother that they could both stop their hard work now. She wanted to let them know that everything was going to be all right. In fact, things were much better already. The pain was completely gone.

All she felt was a kind of warm and happy peace. It was like being surrounded by the light of love. She'd never felt such warmth and love before. She loved her mother, even though she did think that her mother shouldn't have said all those horrible things to her. Ella forgave her mother for all the ugly words. The words didn't matter anymore. She was finished with all that.

She already knew that none of her mother's mean-spirited words were true. God does not make a woman have more pain to punish her for her sin. He is a loving God and her pain had nothing to do with what she had done.

She loved Missy for trying so hard to stop the bleeding. Missy had cared for her for most of her life. It was almost as if she'd had two mothers. Whenever she was tired, afraid, or even sick, Missy was the one she always ran to for comfort. Missy sang to her about Jesus and Going to the Promised Land. Missy picked her up when she fell down. Perhaps it was part of the reason that she went so easily into Raymond's embrace. Her parents held her at arm's length throughout her whole life, and the dark-skinned servants were the ones who had held her close when she needed to be held. Ella wanted to tell Missy that it was all right now and she could stop trying so hard. It wasn't working. There was no more reason to worry. Everything was the way it was supposed to be.

She forgave Raymond for leaving her behind when he ran off to see the world. He didn't know he'd left her with a baby. She hoped that he was enjoying his travels and seeing all the exciting things that he had hoped to see. They both knew before he left that there was no way for them to stay together so he had no reason to think that she would have gone along with him. The truth was that if he had asked her, she might have thrown her clothes into a bag and followed him wherever he went. Her mother would have been angry, but then she was angry anyway, so it may have been easier not to have lived with that anger over the past few months. But he had not asked.

Even though Ella was fine now, the time had come for her to go. The beckoning light was warm and bright even though it didn't hurt her eyes at all. She could see someone waiting for her farther down the lighted path, with a hand held out toward her and calling her name. The shadowy figure looked like Aunt Catherine, but then Aunt Catherine was dead. *Am I dead?* She thought. Someone who looked like her father was there waiting with the lady who looked like Aunt Catherine.

"Follow the light, Ella," the shadowy person called out to her. "Keep walking down the path and follow the light. We are here to guide you home."

Ella took a few more steps on the path to reach the shadowy figures but suddenly thought about her baby. She couldn't go away now and leave her baby alone. She knew her mother would not want him. Someone had to take care of her child. She'd heard Missy say she had a son. She'd gotten her wish. Missy had said he was a fine little man. She'd been so exhausted that she never even saw his face. She wondered if he looked like his father or if he resembled the Bledsoes. It didn't matter. He was hers. She loved him. To her, he would be beautiful and perfect. Missy had wrapped him in the rough homemade blankets and put him in the bureau drawer exactly as they had planned. *He needs me to love him and take care of him. I finally have someone who will love and need me...someone of my very own. I won't be lonely anymore. He has to have a name,* she thought. *I have to go back for my baby.*

She quickly turned around and walked back the way she'd come, trying to retrace her steps to find her way back to her baby, but the misty fog swirled around her feet and enveloped her completely and she could not find the path going backwards. She could still hear someone calling her name in the distance. The voices told her to go back to the light, but she couldn't find it.

She called out, "Papa, Aunt Catherine, I can't come with you. I have a baby now, a son, and I want to stay with him. He needs me."

The light and the path were gone, swallowed up in the swirling clouds. She kept walking in the mist, searching for the path of light for what seemed like a very long time. She heard the voices getting farther and farther away and tried to follow the sound. Finally, the voices were gone and there was no one to ask for help. Ella didn't know what to do. She could have been walking in circles for all she knew. There were no landmarks or voices from that end to guide her back to her body. She was left to wander on her own with no idea of where to go or what to do next. She felt lost and a little bit afraid.

Rita grabbed her daughter in her arms and begged, "Come back to me, Ella; please don't die and leave me alone. I forgive you for what you did. I swear I do. I am sorry that I said those things. God forgives you too; I know that he does. I will pray for you. Please, dear Jesus, don't take my daughter away from me. She's all I have. Please forgive her for what she did and let her stay with me. I need you, Ella, I need you and I want you to stay with me... Please, Lord Jesus, please don't take her away from me. I'm begging you."

She held her daughter tightly to her chest, rocking and moaning with grief, and then suddenly shook her so hard that her head flopped back and forth. She demanded that the girl wake up and not die. She let her fall back against the pillows, slapped the girl's pale cheeks, and rubbed her cold hands to warm them, but nothing worked.

Missy knew that the girl's spirit was gone. She felt it leave. One minute her heart was beating and the next minute that same heart was still. The blood still dripped from the bed clothes to the floor, but it was quiet like the raindrops dripping from the trees after the storm is over.

There was nothing left there on the cot but an empty shell. Missy prayed for God to take the girl into heaven and told Him that she was a good girl who'd made a mistake and she hoped that He would not count it against her.

The grieving mother howled sorrowfully like a wounded animal, taking the remains of her only child into her arms and rocking back and forth again. Missy tried to pull her away to offer her comfort, but the woman pushed her away and seemed inconsolable.

Rita lowered Ella's lifeless body to the mattress and began pulling her own hair and clothing and then curled herself into a ball on the floor beside her daughter's bed. Missy had never seen her cry before. It was sad and made her see Mrs. Bledsoe in a whole new light. Maybe the woman had not gone as cold inside as she'd thought. She might have been upset with Ella for the pregnancy, but she loved her and would certainly miss the girl.

Grief in this case was a natural reaction, so Missy let her be, and began to pick up the clean rags and fold the blankets that had not been used in the delivery. She would take the bloody rags and linens back to her house to wash in the big black pot outside by the woodshed tomorrow.

This was a sorrowful day. There was a lot left to be done. She needed to find a wet-nurse for the baby and she had to clean up Miss Ella's body and figure out what to do about the burying. She was not sure how Mrs. Bledsoe was going to deal with the preacher.

Chapter Ten

As she worked, Missy watched Mrs. Bledsoe and looked at Ella lying there. It was such a sad way for the day to end up. She had hoped to see Ella holding her child by this time. Even if the girl had chosen to give him up, she would have wanted to hold him and see that he was all right. The memories ran around inside her head. Miss Ella had been five years old when the family first moved to Whittington Plantation. Old Mr. Whittington was proud as a peacock and bragged about his new Yankee Farm Manager to anybody who'd listen. When the new man arrived, the locals found Mr. Bledsoe was a quiet man but had a lot of fancy ideas about farming and was very much against the idea of slavery. He said a lot of highfalutin' things that nobody understood except him and Mr. Whittington – he said words like Social Reformation and Racial Harmony and Equality in the eyes of God. Most of the locals both white and colored thought he was just another crazy Yankee. The old overseer that had been there when the war started had run off to join the local Negro militia and ended up in a Yankee prison camp where they'd heard that he died from a fever before the war was over. He'd been a good man but the farm suffered when he left and there were some who claimed that he had abandoned them all. Many of the freed slaves had little faith in the idea of freedom and felt like everything would just go back to the way it was as soon as the war ended. Most of them never believed true freedom could happen and didn't really know what it meant. Some of them moved away.

Mr. Whittington had always been good to his slaves; in fact, most all of them, like Missy's family, stayed close by even after the war. They did the same jobs as they had when they were slaves but now they got paid for them. The government gave each freed male slave forty acres of land and a mule. It was enough to feed their families and make enough crops to give a share back to the Whittingtons. They had a hard time tending their crops and working for the plantation too, but they got by. Mr. Whittington wanted to try Mr. Bledsoe's new agricultural ideas. He said it would make it easier on all of them. Most of the workers couldn't tell much difference.

None of the workers understood it. Mr. Whittington had stood up on the stump by the big barn and talked way above their heads but they knew enough to see that to him and Mr. Bledsoe, it would be a grand experiment. Most of them didn't want to be anybody's experiment. All they wanted was a good wage for a good day's work and to be left alone to work their own places without getting a beating if something didn't go right. They didn't want to have the white bosses involved in their lives but it was going to take some time until they learned to live without it. They had a lot to learn about self-reliance but they were doing it, bit by bit. That word "freedom" might have a fancy ring to it but mostly it meant they had been cut loose from the only security they'd ever known and had to find their own way in a world they were not equipped to deal with.

Missy wondered what Mr. Bledsoe would have said about equality and racial harmony if he'd been around to get a look at his new grandson. Most of the white men that she knew would have torn the whole county apart looking for the man at fault. Then they'd have seen to it that the man was beaten to death or hung from the nearest tree. But then, Mr. Bledsoe was different. It was hard to guess what the man would have said or done. Ella seemed to think her father would have understood.

Missy's sister, who worked at the Plantation house, said Mr. Whittington hired Mr. Bledsoe with a letter in the mail without even having met the man. He told everybody that the old-fashioned ways were on their way out and Whittington Plantation was going to be the biggest producing farm in Alabama one day. His attitude and bragging were not very popular with the other local farmers, who didn't do so well during the war years. Some of the big plantations had been overrun by Yankee troops or even burned and would take years to rebuild and get back to growing anything.

All of that big talk probably helped to set the Bledsoe family up for being mistreated from the start. They were Yankees, after all, probably hated by some of the blacks and the whites before they even got to town. Up north both him and her were s'posed to be from big rich families and they tried to hold onto that family pride even though Missy knew now that Mr. Bledsoe had torn their lives apart and dragged them down to Alabama for reasons of his own. The fact that they were better dressed than other overseers' families in the area didn't help them fit in, nor did their Yankee accents or Mrs. Bledsoe's uppity attitude toward their neighbors. Mr. Bledsoe acted like a gentleman and called himself a Farm Manager rather than using the awful job title of Overseer like the others in his job still did. And he expected to be treated like a gentleman too. The other overseers laughed at him behind his back and said that he didn't know what he was talking about. They said that the man could take his crazy Yankee farming ideas and go back up north where he belonged. They saw him as a threat to their own way of living and said nobody who farmed in Pennsylvania would know diddly-squat about farming in Alabama. She heard one of the older men say that the Yankee didn't know the difference between a Piss-ant and a Boll-Weevil and all those around him had laughed at his joke and agreed that he was probably right.

Missy's brother Joe said they ought to give it a chance before saying how crazy it was. He liked the man and tried to learn from him. Missy didn't care much one way or another. Nothing he ever said made any difference in the way she grew her own tomatoes, sweet corn, and turnip greens.

She didn't like Mrs. Bledsoe all that much but she did learn to care about Ella. The child was quiet and hung around with Missy and Slimmy because there wasn't anybody else to talk to. She'd even help with the chores when her mother wasn't looking, just for something to do. She never raised her voice or caused a fuss, and she ate the food that was put on her plate without complaining. The poor child never had a chance at fitting into society down here.

Only two family members came to visit during the whole eleven years they lived in Alabama. The first was Mr.

Bledsoe's brother, William, who came to get some business papers signed. He stayed for a few days and everybody was glad to see him leave, especially Missy and Joe and Slimmy. He didn't crack a smile the whole time. He whined about the heat and the humidity, and the food was not to his liking. He got all upset and said he was appalled at what he called the attitudes of the people he met at the train station when he arrived. Missy didn't know for sure what it meant to be appalled but she figured it had to be bad. He started bad-mouthing the South as soon as he got to the plantation. That seemed to be the wrong way to make anyone like you, or so it seemed to Missy.

He said people in the South had certainly changed after the war. In the city, you could still easily find a porter. He had trouble finding a carriage to drive him out to the plantation and then they took him to the big house on the hill instead of his brother's place. He was upset by the fact that his brother had been out in a field with the field hands tending to the cotton when he arrived and had forgotten to go to the station in spite of the letter that he had sent ahead to tell him his arrival time. Mr. Bledsoe apologized and told him that they had not received any letter or notice of any kind about his visit, and then everybody tried to make him feel welcome. They argued that night at the dinner table. He said that John and Rita had forgotten their place in society and were living like second-class trash. The man had even asked Mrs. Bledsoe why none of the servants wore proper uniforms. Mrs. Bledsoe had said that she didn't feel that uniforms were necessary in a well-run household, and then the two men had picked at each other throughout the whole dinner. No one was sorry when his business was done and he left to go back up north where they felt he belonged.

It was obvious even to Slimmy and Missy that the older brother did not approve of the younger brother's new situation. He probably had plenty of bad talk for the relatives when he got back home.

The other visitor was Mr. Bledsoe's sister Catherine. She was a very quiet and pretty lady who had planned to stay for several months but had gotten really sick and passed away less than two weeks after her arrival. The doctor said it had been some kind of fever, but nobody else caught it, so he said there was a chance that she had been ill when she arrived. The family up north did not believe that. They blamed Mr. Bledsoe for luring her down to this God-forsaken place to catch a fever and die. Her brother buried her in the family plot behind the house instead of paying to have her coffin shipped back up north. That made them angry. After that, Mrs. Bledsoe stopped talking about having visitors and began to talk only of going home.

Mr. Bledsoe was so depressed over his sister's death that he spent two solid days locked up in his study with nothing but a bottle of whiskey and a glass. Then on the third day he went to his room, where he bathed and dressed and went back to the fields to work and never mentioned the situation again. Missy and Slimmy had both thought it was the strangest reaction to someone's dying that either of them had ever seen or heard of before. Mrs. Bledsoe had kept to her rooms and didn't talk to anyone either. Missy knew that she'd been fond of the lady and was sorry to lose her company. She'd been really happy to have Miss Catherine come to visit. In fact, she had been a much more pleasant person during the visit until the lady became ill. They all felt a little sorry for her after that. She was like a catfish out of water down here. She breathed but struggled to survive. Her face began to change into a mask of sad acceptance.

Ella had been her mother's pride and joy when she was younger. The little girl was shy and a little clumsy. She wasn't as dainty or as prissy as some of the other plantation girls, but her mother seemed to adore her. She was taught good manners and all the things a lady needed to know throughout her life. Mrs. Bledsoe bought her the most stylish clothes, even though the ribbons, ruffles, and lace looked to be very uncomfortable. Missy and Slimmy spent hours over hot irons to make the clothes look neat and crisp but after a short time in the Alabama heat and humidity, the dresses drooped and sagged on the hangers. They'd spend time every day dressing the girl and doing her hair as if they were expecting company, even though there weren't any white children her age and social status to call friends or playmates. She'd be dressed, her hair would be done, and then she would have to sit quietly for the rest of the day.

The only times the women left home were for occasional trips to the general store and on those days, they would eat lunch at the only restaurant in town. They went to church a few times when they first arrived but Mrs. Bledsoe soon decided the local Methodist minister was not preaching the true word and refused to go anymore. Missy had heard from one of her sisters who worked at the big Whittington house that Mrs. Bledsoe had gotten upset because there was no special pew in the church set aside for them as the Whittingtons' Farm Manager's family like there was for the owners of the Plantation. None of the other overseers had special pews, so the poor old minister hadn't even thought about it. She complained and said that she would not be back until the situation was remedied. Missy's sister said the minister went to the big house that very day and asked Mr. Whittington about getting them a pew of their own and he ordered the new pew for them from the same local woodworker who had made the rest of the church pews. They moved a regular pew into place for the family until the new one was made, but the family never went back to church to use it. The new hand-built pew with its placard on the side reading "Farm Manager and Family" sat empty every Sunday from then on.

The family never went to visit anyone local and the locals never came to visit them. Ella was never allowed to go outside to run and play freely as the rest of the plantation children were. Every time she did go out, she was told, "Don't get your dress dirty, Ella. Don't pick that up, Ella, it's dirty. Watch where you step, Ella, don't get dirt on your stockings."

One day Missy felt so sorry for the child that she had told Mrs. Bledsoe that she'd be happy to save some flour sacks to make Ella a few simple little dresses to play in. Mrs. Bledsoe said that Ella did not need play clothes and if she did, she wasn't going to have her daughter wearing dresses made of flour sacks. It was funny though that when the baby was on the way, flour sacks were perfectly all right for making blankets for him. Most every child Missy knew wore clothes made out of flour sacks. Missy's own dresses except for the rare hand-me-downs from donations given to the church were made from them. They might not be the latest fashion but she fit in with everyone she knew and none of them felt slighted. They used to trade pieces of material to help each other get the right designs to make their simple dresses, or they'd mix the designs and make them even more cheerful.

The girl's father ignored her most of the time until she was old enough to go out riding with him. He was so wrapped up in his own work that for days at a time he never seemed to notice that the girl was around. When she tried to talk to him, she was promptly sent away to find something else to do.

Ella said that getting her horse, Maggie, for her tenth birthday was the greatest thing that had happened in her whole life. Ella spent hours in the barn talking to Maggie and brushing and caring for the animal. Missy had never owned a horse like that. She and her family had mules that worked for their living. But she was glad that Ella had Maggie to keep her busy. She'd never thought much about an animal being a friend, but in Ella's case, it seemed to be a good thing and she tried to understand it. The poor girl had to have something to care about and keep her mind and her hands occupied.

Mr. Bledsoe never seemed to have much time for his wife either. Missy wasn't trying to be nosey, but it seemed like they were not very close. They never smiled or touched one another like Mr. and Mrs. Whittington did, but then Mrs. Bledsoe was always worrying about what was ladylike, so Missy never knew what they were like when no one was around. They had no social life. There were other plantations in the area, but the overseers were either black men or rough-looking white men who Mrs. Bledsoe claimed were lower class. They did give a dinner party soon after their arrival, but it hadn't gone well. She and Mrs. Bledsoe spent a week getting the menu planned and preparing the food. Missy had even gotten special recipes from her sister at the big house to make sure the food was grand.

Mrs. Bledsoe said that the wives of the other farm managers came dressed like saloon girls and were not ladies at all. They even acted like saloon girls. One of the wives told a naughty story at the dinner table that made both Mr. and Mrs. Bledsoe blush clean up to their hairlines. After dinner another of the wives discovered the piano in the front room and sat down to play without even asking permission and soon struck up a bawdy song that had all the drunken menfolk laughing and singing at the top of their lungs. Mrs. Bledsoe got upset and had her husband send them away as quickly as possible and stomped up the stairs to her room to read her bible. Missy and Slimmy cleaned up after the party and figured that was the last dinner party at the Farm Manager's house.

Mrs. Bledsoe refused to associate with the other farm managers or their families after that. The farm managers said that she thought she was better than everyone else and they didn't want to be friends with her anyway.

Missy thought Mr. Bledsoe was even odder than most of the white men she'd met. She thought that it probably had something to do with him being a Yankee. He talked to Joe and the other workers, but never had much to say to Missy and Slimmy except to ask for something or to thank them when he got it. He was usually gone during the day but at home he spent a lot of time at his desk, with big books and what he called "his charts" piled up around him. He smoked thin little cigars and sipped whiskey from his crystal glasses.

One night he keeled over, face down on his desk. Slimmy found him the next morning when she went to ask if he wanted a breakfast tray. He was already gone stone cold and stiff. Slimmy'd gone to Mrs. Bledsoe's room and helped her get dressed before she went to the study to see it for herself. They sent for the doctor but there was nothing to be done by that time. They ordered up a casket, had a funeral, and buried him in the plot beside his sister all in a matter of a couple of days. All the workers came to stand at the graveside. The minister apologized for not knowing how to conduct a Quaker funeral. Missy didn't know what a Quaker was, but figured a Methodist funeral was probably good enough for most anybody. She'd never seen any other kind. She and Slimmy and some of the workers even shed a few tears.

After the death of her husband, Mrs. Bledsoe said that Miss Ella was all she had left to live for and she wanted the two of them to go back home. The two of them only planned to stay in Alabama until the summer when they could get back to living what Mrs. Bledsoe called a "normal" life up north. Her eyes lit up when she said that there would be parties where Ella could meet young people of her own age and social position. She said they'd go straight to the dressmakers when they arrived and order new clothes for them both. There'd be so many exciting things to do, like going for carriage rides in the parks and visiting with friends. And best of all, come winter, there would be snow...beautiful white snow covering everything and turning the whole city into a wintry dreamland for the holiday season. She talked about the lavish decorations that her family would have put out and the different foods they would eat for Christmas dinner. Going home was all they could talk about until Miss Ella started losing her breakfast every morning and Missy realized that Ella was pregnant. She kept the thought to herself until she noticed she was growing through the middle. She finally sat the girl down at the kitchen table and asked her some very personal and embarrassing questions. Ella was so innocent that she still hadn't believed she was going to have a baby until it began to kick.

From that day on, she'd been happy about the baby and asked all kinds of questions about how to be a mother. Missy answered her questions and taught her to make blankets and little gowns and diapers for the child to wear when it finally arrived. They had to talk quietly though. Mrs. Bledsoe hated hearing them talking about anything to do with the baby and would launch into one of her religious screaming fits if they got her riled up.

The day they told Mrs. Bledsoe about the new situation, she was furious. She called that young girl ugly names that even Missy had never heard. She was mostly upset because it was going to spoil their trip back to Pennsylvania. She was also mad because she could not get any information about the father out of her daughter. She ranted and raved and poor Ella cried and remained stubbornly silent. Now they would never know who the father was. Perhaps it was better that way.

Chapter Eleven

Missy sighed deeply and turned around to add a folded blanket to the stack on the trunk beside her, and saw Mrs. Bledsoe getting up on her wobbly knees. She thought the woman was trying to stand up. But, instead, the woman angrily snatched up the sleeping baby from the makeshift bed in the bureau drawer. Before Missy could drop the blanket and run the few steps across the room to stop her, the distraught woman raised the infant high above her head and slammed him onto the floor with all the strength of her hatred and anger and grief. Her eyes were bulging and the veins stood out in her neck as she picked him up to do it again.

She yelled, "Oh God, NO! Mrs. Bledsoe, you cain't do that!" She wrestled with the woman to get the limp bundle out of her hands, but she jumped up on her feet, turned sideways, and crashed the baby onto the top of the marble-topped dressing table with all her strength. She pushed out at Missy so hard that both of them fell backwards and landed on their backsides on the floor. Missy grabbed onto the bedpost and pulled herself up to her knees.

Tears flowed down both their cheeks as they glared at each other. They had known each other for eleven long years. They were not friends and never would be, but they knew each other well. Missy stumbled over, took the baby from Rita's grip, and knew immediately from the stillness that the newborn was already dead. His eyes were closed and there was blood seeping from his ears and nose. She wrapped him up in the flour sack blanket and laid him carefully on the top of the dresser.

The tears welled up in her big brown eyes. That poor child never had a chance. She hoped that God would know that. He was so new that he had never even tasted his mother's milk. Surely, God had a special place for an innocent child.

Missy yelled, "You done kilt it, Mrs. Bledsoe. You done kilt it dead. How could you do that? It weren't his fault. He was an innocent chile."

Mrs. Bledsoe looked up at her with so much ugliness in her face that Missy felt as if she had been physically slapped.

"Innocent? He was not innocent! That little bastard killed my daughter. He ripped her up inside and killed her as sure as if he had cut her with a knife! If I could find the man who did this, I would strangle him with my bare hands. He put that bastard in my daughter and now she is gone. Somebody has to pay for that!"

Her knees gave way and she fell down again on the floor, holding onto a bloody sheet and crying out her grief and her misery. It was the most pitiful thing that Missy had ever witnessed in her whole life. She didn't like the woman all that much and she hated what she had done to that child, but she did understand her pain.

Missy wrung her hands and muttered to herself, "Oh Lord, what a mess. Sweet Jesus, what am I going to do 'bout this? Somethin' surely has to be done, and I ain't got no idea of where to start."

It was time to get practical. There were two dead bodies to deal with and a woman so grief stricken that she was capable of almost anything. Missy didn't know what to expect from Mrs. Bledsoe. She might lie quietly and cry or she could turn violent and try to kill herself or even attack Missy. The tears dripped down her cheeks as she went over the options. She was so afraid that her heart nearly pounded through her chest.

Chapter Twelve

Missy decided to leave them as they were. The dead girl was lying in her bed, and the babe was dead on the dresser top, still loosely bundled in his sad little flour sack blankets. The grandmother was once again rocking and weeping on the floor beside her daughter's bed. Missy realized the damage was already done and the dead ones were beyond her help.

Missy turned from the grisly scene and ran down the stairs and out the back door. She looked back once to reassure herself that Mrs. Bledsoe was likely to stay put for a few minutes and then jumped down the wooden steps and cut through the rows of the large vegetable garden toward her brother Joe, on the other side. Her brother was older and she felt sure that he would help her do what had to be done. He'd been in the war and learned about pain and death. He knew how to handle things and she trusted his common sense and quiet strength. At that point, she needed her brother's help and she needed it fast.

She could hear him chopping wood behind the house they'd shared since their parents had died. She yelled at him as she ran barefooted down the row between the okra and tomato plants.

"Joe, come here quick! You gotta help me! Hurry! You gotta come now."

Joe took off his beat-up old hat with one hand, took out his sweat-soaked handkerchief with the other, wiped his dripping face and neck, and watched his sister stumble toward him out of the garden. She was holding her blood-soaked housedress and apron above her knobby knees to make it easier to run. He had expected her to come and tell him whether the baby was a boy or a girl, but she looked much too upset to be coming for that. In fact, he had never seen her look so messy or covered in blood. Something was bad wrong.

"Calm youself, woman," he called. "I cain't understand a word you sayin'. Take a breath and tell me what's the matter."

Missy finally got close enough to be understood and braced her hands on her knees while bending over to catch her breath. Her headache was throbbing with every heartbeat. She began to tell him the story, talking so fast that he had to listen carefully to get it all.

"Joe, I don' know what to do but we gotta do sumptin, now! Miss Ella had her baby a while ago and he was a Negro baby, Joe, and then she started bleedin' and I couldn' make the bleedin' stop and she jes' up and died! It was jes' pourin' out of her by the cupful. They's blood all over the floor. I don't know how we gone get all that blood cleaned up. It looks like a hog's been butchered in there. Oh Lord, Joe, I hope that it wasn't because I gave her some willow bark tea.

It's s'posed to cut the pain but Mama said that it had to be used real careful, 'cause it might make the bleeding worse. Joe, she was hurtin' so bad, and I didn't know any other way to make it better. Oh God, Joe, I didn't mean to do nothing that woulda hurt that pore girl. I swear I didn't. It was terrible, Joe, It was 'bout de worstest thang I ever seen! And then Mrs. Bledsoe...she was hollerin' and cryin' and layin' in the floor and afore I knowed what was happ'nin' she done grabbed up that pore little baby boy and raised him up over her head and smashed him onto the floor and then she cracked his head on the dressing table and she kilt him, Joe, she done kilt him dead! Oh sweet Jesus...that pore little baby boy, she done kilt him dead. He was so purty, Joe, I coulda found him a mama who'da taken him in with no trouble a'tall. I was thinkin' that me and you could raise him up even if I couldn't find him a mama. Don't you think we could have?"

She covered her tear-stained face with shaking hands and sobbed out her own shock and sadness.

Joe asked, "Where's Slimmy? What's she doing?"

"Slimmy went home after we cleaned up the kitchen. Mrs. Bledsoe didn't want nobody but me and her around when the baby was born. She's trying to keep this thing a big ole secret like anybody around here would even care 'bout what Miss Ella had done. Besides that, Slimmy was saying that Miss Ella's hollering was givin' her a headache. It was giving us all headaches but, Joe, that li'l ole gal was sufferin' so much. I couldn't stand watchin' her go through it. That's why I gave her the willow bark tea. I wished I hadn't done it. I wish it with all my heart. Ohhh Lord, I hope I didn't kill that girl. I won't never git over it if I did."

Hearing a story like that was enough to get Joe moving. He took a deep cleansing breath, plopped his sweaty old hat back on his head, stuck his damp handkerchief back in his pocket, and headed back through the rows of vegetables growing in the garden. He looked back at his sister, who was wiping her face with her bloodstained apron. "Well, sister, you comin? Sounds to me like we got us a job to do. We best be getting to it. We don't want to leave Mrs. Bledsoe in there by herself too long. No tellin' what she'll think of doing next. And, sister, you don't be sayin' nothing more about giving that girl no willow bark tea or nothing else you mighta done. I know you done your best. Nobody can ask for no better than that. So you stop frettin' about dat. You hear me? Whatever happened was God's will, you know dat."

She stood there shaking and took one more deep breath while looking into her brother's sad brown eyes, and then broke into a run and caught up with him. Joe was a strong man and having him there to help her was going to make things go better for sure.

"I didn't know what to do, Joe, there's two dead bodies in there and Mrs. Bledsoe, she was actin' crazy. She was ahowlin' like a dog and layin' on dat floor. I never seen or heard nothin' like it. It was scary but it was so sad, Joe, so sad that it would purely break your heart."

"Come on, sister, I done told you, we gone do the best we can. That's all we can do. There was no way that any of this could have ended up good. You know it," he reminded her. "We knew when Miss Ella done turned up pregnant that there was gone be trouble of some kind. We jes' gotta take it as it comes, one step at a time."

They stopped at the Bledsoes' tool shed, got a shovel and a bucket, and kept on going.

They went into the back door and straight up to the room where Missy had left them all. Joe took off his beat-up ole hat and looked around. Mrs. Bledsoe was still in a heap on the floor. She was silent now except for the sniffles and an occasional hiccup. She was staring into space with sad, wide eyes and was clenching and un-clenching her hands while holding onto a blanket. Miss Ella's body was laying there on her bed as still as a rock. Her nightdress was covered in blood and there was a lake of it pooled under the bed. It was an awful sight and with the heat, the room smelled as bad as it looked. He opened up the double windows to let the place air out. The copper penny smell of blood began to dissipate rapidly even without a breeze. No wonder his sister looked wild eyed and frazzled. The scene before him was enough to make anybody go frazzled.

Chapter Thirteen

Missy wondered what the sobbing woman was thinking but then decided that she didn't want to know. Some pain was so private that a body wouldn't want to share it or hear it. And she couldn't get over the fact that Mrs. Bledsoe had actually killed that poor little child. That was one little young'un that never had a chance from the moment he was born. She prayed that Lord Jesus would take that innocent child into his arms and give him some peace. Then she asked for a little of that peace for herself. The sight of Mrs. Bledsoe slamming the baby down on the floor and dresser top was likely to make her have nightmares for years to come. She understood grief, but murder went way beyond the normal reaction to grief, and it made her insides churn and her knees go weak to remember it.

Missy and Joe picked up the sobbing woman with one of them on each arm, walked her slowly down the stairs and toward the kitchen, and managed to get her seated in a ladder-backed chair at the kitchen table. Missy poured a cup of coffee and added a heaping spoon of brown cane sugar to the cup. She held it up to Mrs. Bledsoe's mouth to have her take a sip. Rita took the cup in her own shaky hands and took a drink. She closed her eyes and held the coffee in her mouth for a second or two before swallowing it.

"That's good coffee, Missy. Did you make it? You always did make a good cup of coffee," she said quietly after a few seconds and then opened her eyes.

Missy had not made the coffee. It was some of what was left from the pot that Slimmy had made before she left to go home hours ago, but she didn't think it was worth correcting the woman.

Missy took off her bloodstained apron and sat in a chair across the table from her employer. She wanted to offer comfort but was so overwrought herself that she wasn't sure of what to say. She said, "You gone be all right, Mrs. Bledsoe. We gone figure out somethin' that'll make it right."

The woman said softly, "It's never going to be all right again, Missy." She unpinned her sweat-soaked hair and ran her fingers through it and then twisted it back into a bun on the back of her head and re-pinned it the same way that Missy had seen her do so many times over the past eleven years.

Then she calmly started talking about the laundry that would have to be done. She told Missy that she was to take the dirty linens to her own house to do them because she never wanted to see any of it again. Missy agreed to do as she wished. She was planning to do that anyway, but she didn't want to make an issue of the matter, so she said, "Yes, ma'am" and nodded her head.

The laundry would have to wait. Before Missy took time to deal with laundry there were more important things to be handled. She looked across the kitchen to see Joe heading back upstairs to the dead girl's room to begin dealing with the worst of them.

Missy and Mrs. Bledsoe talked quietly and calmly almost as though none of the events of the past few hours had ever happened.

Rita told her with a loud sigh, "I am going to put all of this behind me and go home where I belong. I see now that I should never have agreed to come to this place with my husband."

She picked up the tea towel that she had spent many hours embroidering blue flowers on and began to wipe her sweaty face. "You know, Mr. Bledsoe was a very dedicated man who was concerned about the after-effects of the years of slavery and he felt obligated to come down here and help to put things right after the hateful practice was eliminated. He was a good man, a hard-working man. He wanted to show all you southerners that a man could run a farm successfully without having slaves. He wanted to make things better for your people. Most of you didn't understand what he was trying to do for you. I could tell that from the way you all treated us. The sad part was that he thought it was working well. He ignored the snide remarks and the ugly looks that people gave him. He believed in what he was trying to accomplish. He truly believed it was the right thing to do.

"It was right around harvest time when he started having the pains in his head from time to time. There was so much to do after the fire. We thought it was just headaches because of the heat and his working too hard. The doctor told him he needed to rest more. He didn't rest. He said there was too much work to be done for him to take time out to rest. He died and left us here in this place, so far away from our home and family. I do wish he hadn't done that.

"Missy, I hated this place from the very first day I saw it. I hated the heat, the humidity, and the odors. I hated the people. Every time we went out, we could feel their eyes on us. I wanted to go home. Mr. Bledsoe said that it was important that Ella and I stay here with him and present a united front. He said the people would grow to like us as time went on. They never did as far as I could tell. I never learned to like them either. Now, it doesn't matter much to me whether they liked us or not. I'm going home alone, and three of the people I cared most about in my life are buried out there in that hateful red clay behind this ugly little house. After I get settled, I might consider paying to have their bodies brought up north and placed in the family burial plots where they should rightfully be. Yes, that is an excellent idea. I will do that as quickly as I can afford it. Maybe John's father would pay to have that done. I will go home and then have my husband and my daughter and my best friend's bodies exhumed and moved back home with me where we all belong. I don't want to leave any of my loved ones in this God-forsaken place a moment longer than I have to."

Having Mrs. Bledsoe talk to her that way was very strange but it was better than seeing her the way she had been a little while before. She seemed to have gone into a state of scary calmness. She talked more to Missy, sitting at the table that day, than ever before in all the years they had known each other.

Chapter Fourteen

Joe went back into Ella's room timidly wiping his face with his handkerchief and feeling like a trespasser. Her papa had been his boss and Joe'd respected him and his family. He'd thought Mr. Bledsoe had some funny ideas and talked a lot about the stuff he'd read in his big books about farming. Neither Joe, the other workers, nor even the other overseers had ever heard of books like that before. None of them were educated men and they didn't trust what they called book-learnin'. Mr. Bledsoe never did see that farming up north was different from farming in south Alabama, but overall, he was a good man. He treated the colored people on the farm the same way he treated anyone else, and that made the workers who took the time to get to know him like him.

The other local overseers didn't understand his ways of farming and especially didn't agree with his ideas about treating the workers the same as anyone else. According to their way of thinking, the workers were all ignorant, lazy, and would do only enough to get by, no matter how well they were treated. There was one man, Manny Green from

Seven Pines Plantation down the road a few miles, who insisted that there was nothing like a public beating to get the workers to produce more. He still carried a rolled-up whip on his saddle and had been known to use it in spite of the new laws put into place to protect the rights of the freed slaves.

Mr. Bledsoe hadn't liked the man.

Since the Bledsoes' arrival, Joe had worked as a tenant farmer and general laborer. It had been a good arrangement and they had all managed to get what they needed and a little bit extra. For the first time in his life, Joe had money put aside. He was grateful and felt good about his life as a free person of color.

Joe had not known Ella nearly as well as his sister Missy and cousin Slimmy did. Still, entering the room where the girl had given birth and died a short time before had a very big impact on his emotions. The girl had never been unkind to him. They saw each other fairly often as they moved around the farm each day. He always lowered his eyes when she spoke to him and even if she didn't acknowledge him, he nodded his head and touched the front of his beat-up old hat anyway as a show of respect.

He looked at her lying there with her pale skin and slack face. She looked like she was sleeping. She had been kind of pretty when she smiled. Her eyes sort of lighted up and there was a hint of personality there that he didn't see very often. He didn't think of himself as an expert on pretty women of any race; however, he had noticed that she never had friends come to visit and the young gentlemen did not come calling the way they had called on Miss Amy Whittington when she lived in the big plantation house down the road. But then, Miss Amy Whittington was known far and wide as a beauty with her flashing eyes and feminine ways.

When she married, there were so many people at the wedding that they couldn't fit all the horses in the barns. The Negro help had stayed with friends and some even slept in the stalls with their owners' horses. The people were sharing rooms and sleeping on cots, and the children slept on pallets on the floor. It had been the first big plantation wedding since the war and everyone had wanted to be a part of it. They had baked two wedding cakes and passed out slices of cake to everybody there, including the workers who had showed up on that day. It had been good cake too. Joe loved sweets. The Bledsoes had not been invited but they sent a gift anyway. Joe had thought that was nice of them.

He'd always felt a little bit sorry for Miss Ella. She was like a young colt...all elbows and knees sometimes. The poor girl was timid and seemed uncomfortable around people other than her own family or the servants, but then she didn't often see anyone else. Her mama was always pushing her to be more girly and telling her to stand up straighter and behave more like a lady. Mrs. Bledsoe made her try to do needlework and read books aloud while they sat out in the garden, but it seemed to Joe that the girl did not enjoy those things. He was as surprised as everyone else when the girl turned up pregnant. Such a possibility had never entered his mind. She just didn't seem to be the kind of girl that would end up that way.

The only times he saw Ella look truly happy was when she was riding that horse of hers. He and Mr. Bledsoe had picked Maggie for Ella's tenth birthday. The girl had been thrilled with her gift. She had made Joe show her how to brush the animal and feed her and she'd spend hours in the barn taking care of her. After she got a few years older, she'd put on a pair of her daddy's old britches and ride that mare like a demon. She always rode alone unless her daddy was with her. She probably knew every inch of Whittington Plantation and then some. He had seen her jump across the creek and lie down on the neck of that horse and run flat out until both she and the horse were exhausted. He worried sometimes that she was pushing the animal too hard, but when the run was over, the girl would take her horse to the spring for a cool drink of water and they'd walk around and cool down before they made their way back more slowly to the barn. It appeared that they both needed the run, and the mare never behaved in any way to suggest that she felt abused. That horse was fast and Ella seemed to love the speed as much as Maggie did.

If things had been different, Joe might have even suggested to Mr. Bledsoe that that mare would make a good racehorse but that was none of his business and he'd never have brought it up. Now that she was gone, he wondered what would happen to the horses. He had a little money saved. He wondered if Mrs. Bledsoe would sell any of them. He'd heard her say that she wanted to go back up north, so he figured she might want to sell all of the livestock. He knew some people who might be interested and he could offer to make a sale for some of the animals in exchange for a small amount from the sales price. There was Mr. Bledsoe's big stallion and Ella's Maggie as well as a set of near matched bays they used to pull the carriage. There were also some beef cattle as well as milk cows and the chickens, ducks, and guinea fowl. If he got a good price, his share would go a long way toward keeping him and his sister in grits and gravy for a while. By some people's measuring he would almost be well off. That would be a good feeling.

But first, there was work to do. He laid his hat on the dresser top and picked out a place to start.

Chapter Fifteen

Joe clumsily picked up the girl's stiffening body and laid her as gently as he could on the flat top of the big trunk under the windowsill. He stripped the bloody linens off the bed, used them to wipe up the puddle of congealing blood, then piled them together in a bundle with the bloody parts hidden inside. A stain was still on the floor where the blood had soaked into the grain of the wood, but he figured he would have to deal with that later. It was hard to believe that one person's body could hold so much. Most of what she'd had inside her had leaked out as far as he could tell. The mattress was covered by a sheet of oilcloth that had protected it from the worst of it. He took that off and wiped it down as well as he could and folded it to give back to his sister. It was part of her birthin' kit and he knew that she would be able to clean it better after she got it back home. She might have her own way of cleaning those things so he put all her stuff together in one place so that she could find it easily.

Joe walked softly to the kitchen door and motioned for Missy to join him. She gave a brief nod, excused herself from the table, and joined him upstairs in Ella's room. He needed to know where the clean linens could be found. Missy got out what was needed from a drawer in the wash table. Together they turned the mattress over, put a clean sheet on the cot, and laid the body of the girl out on the freshened bed.

They moved the bed with its occupant to the other side of the room so that Joe could work on the floor. He saw Mrs. Bledsoe still sitting at the kitchen table as he went outside to get the scrubbing brushes and the homemade lye soap from the tool shed. Then he went back for two buckets of water from the well and tried to eliminate as much of the evidence as he could.

Missy respectfully bathed the girl's lifeless body, washed and brushed her hair, and dressed her in a clean cotton day dress. She arranged her in a position that was as natural looking as possible with her hands crossed at her waist. Joe commented that she looked so peaceful laying there.

Missy nodded her head but couldn't help but remember that it wasn't but a few hours ago that Ella was asking her to cut her belly open and take the baby out. Missy had rebuffed the idea, but now she wondered if doing that would have helped keep the girl alive. If it worked on cows, as Ella had said, then maybe there really was something to the idea. She'd seen her mama sew up a man's leg once when he cut it with a scythe and he healed up all right. Maybe Joe had heard something about those things. He might have even been there when the deed was done.

She also wanted to ask her friend Mona who had moved back home from Natchez and also did some birthin'. She wondered if Mona ever heard of such a thing. Maybe they could talk about different plants and what they did while they were at it. She felt the need to learn more about her calling.

The old white doctor in town was not very generous with knowledge because he imagined what they did as some kind of "negro mumbo-jumbo." She had told him that she prayed a lot during her deliveries, but the old doctor looked down on that too. He'd said prayer did not take the place of knowledge, but then he would not give her the benefit of his knowledge, even though he did admit that he didn't really want to be called out to deliver the Negro babies. He'd go if he was called for but he preferred that the Negroes take care of their own kind.

It was a frustrating situation for the ones who were trying their best to deliver babies and handle the sickness and injuries that happened to their people. He told her once that the free Negroes needed to get together and send a smart young man to medical school and then they'd have their own doctor. Missy could never figure out how he thought a bunch of tenant farmers, house maids, and blacksmiths would be able to afford that. She had to admit that it would be a wonderful thing to see a colored doctor. Maybe it could happen one day.

Joe picked up the small bundle that held the remains of the baby boy as well as the bigger bundle of dirty linens and left out the back door so that Mrs. Bledsoe wouldn't see him go. He dropped the larger wad of sheets and towels to pick up later and picked up the shovel he'd propped by the door and carried the smaller bundle back across the garden plot.

It had been a sad and unsettling day for sure, a day that he and his sister would spend the rest of their lives trying to forget. It was worse than many of his experiences during the war. Some things a body just wished it could unsee.

He found a spot under the big spreading oak tree behind the house he and Missy shared and dug a grave in the sandy red earth between the thick roots. He carefully tucked the tiny body into a wooden box he'd been using to hold old horseshoes in his shed.

He'd always saved the old horseshoes he found and sold them back to the blacksmith down the road for a penny apiece. He dumped the shoes into a small keg. Now he had a better use for the small sturdy box. It was a little cramped, but it was the best he could do at the time. And it was the only wooden box that he had with a lid.

He got a clean rag from the kitchen to wipe away the blood that had drained from the baby's ears and nose and then stood there looking at the tiny face, wondering what happened to babies who died so young and innocent. It seemed like such a senseless death...a waste. A baby certainly had not committed any sin. The poor babe never even had a name. He was a pretty child. It was wrong in so many ways. Burying this tiny baby had to be one of the saddest chores that Joe had ever done.

Joe, like Missy, had wondered who fathered the babe. It was obvious it had been a man of color, but he'd never seen or heard of anyone who might have done the deed, and the tiny face did not resemble anyone that he could remember. It didn't matter to him, because to him, all babies were blessings straight from heaven, but he was curious. Missy said the girl never said. If she were to tell anyone, Joe figured it would have been Missy. He couldn't help but wonder what Mr. Bledsoe would have done or said about it. He'd told everybody that God didn't see people by color. He said

God saw what was in a man's heart. Well, the little one in the box would have certainly been a test for all those fancy words. Mrs. Bledsoe didn't seem to feel the same way as her husband, that was for sure. She murdered the child. For all her hollering about God and sinning, he wondered if she felt any guilt about killing an innocent babe. It wasn't his place to judge the woman, but he knew that murder was wrong and he hoped that she felt plenty guilty. *She would face her judgment when she passed over the river Jordan, but people just shouldn't do things like that no matter how mad they get,* he thought to himself. He'd heard about folks killing somebody while they were under the influence of strong drink or when they were angry at each other but those were adults fighting each other. Innocent children had no place in situations like that. In fact, he had pretty much decided after the war that folks ought not to be killing each other for any reason. After all, the Bible said: *Thou shalt not kill.*

He found a big flat rock that was large enough to act as a marker and rolled it into place at the top of the grave and wished that he knew the proper words to say for the baby. He tried to think of a prayer but was not sure which words would be suitable for this kind of a sad situation, so he improvised.

He asked the Lord Jesus to take this child into his loving care, because he was as innocent as any ever born. He hoped that would be enough. He felt like crying, but had been taught from early childhood that tears were not going to help anything and certainly, they would not help this child now.

He covered the tiny box with soil and patted it down with the back of the shovel. He started to stomp the dirt down with his scuffed old work shoes but because there was a child in there, he couldn't bring himself to step on the grave. The poor child had suffered enough indignity in his short stay on this earth.

After picking up his shovel, he went back to the brick house on the other side of the garden and then to the family cemetery. He had another grave to dig and felt a need to get on with it. Digging a hole that big was hard work but it had a way of keeping his body occupied so that his thoughts got tired and stayed quiet for a while. That suited him fine for the time being. He could have gotten someone to help with the digging but decided against it. It felt better to do the job alone. He didn't want to have to talk about the things that had happened or answer any questions. Even after it got late in the evening, there was enough moonlight to see, so he finished and made his way back home. He drew water from the outside pump to bathe, knowing full well that nothing could wash the events of that day from his mind, but at least he could get rid of the dirt. Two graves in one day. Dirt from a grave was a bad kind of dirt. It stuck to you worse than regular soil from a garden or growing field. He had heard that once and believed it because it was sticking to his skin and clothes and making him itch and sting. He didn't think he'd ever want to be a gravedigger for money. He knew two men from town who did it. Joe had dug enough graves in his lifetime out of necessity. He sure wouldn't want to try to make a living at it. Just thinking about the ghosts was enough to put him off that idea. It was no wonder those two gravediggers he knew stayed drunk a lot. They probably saw a lot of ghosts in their line of work.

Nope. He didn't like the notion of ghosts at all. They were the scariest things he could think of. Once when he was twelve years old, he'd seen a mass of glowing gas down in the swamp and his cousin Willy said it was a ghost of a pirate that had buried treasure out there in the mist. Willy had gotten real quiet for a minute and then yelled "BOO!" and poked at his shoulder with the boat paddle. It had scared him so bad he'd wet his pants and fallen overboard. Willy laughed at him and said there wasn't any such thing as ghosts. Joe wasn't sure. Even so, he couldn't see that tiny baby or Miss Ella as scary ghosts. They were just plain ole sad.

Chapter Sixteen

Missy stayed with Mrs. Bledsoe that night. She'd heated water on the stove and helped the woman bathe and wash her hair. Afterwards they took the lantern into the room where Ella lay still and quiet. Mrs. Bledsoe didn't mention the baby at all, didn't even ask what had happened to his body. She cried for a minute or so and then wiped her eyes with a black-edged handkerchief, kissed her daughter on the forehead, and shuddered all over. Then she took a deep breath, squared her shoulders, and looked Missy straight in the eye.

"Listen to me, Missy, it's important that you understand me. If anyone asks, we're going to say that she fell off her horse. The rest of the story is nobody's business. I don't want you and Slimmy talking about my daughter behind my back. You hear me? Do you understand what I am telling you to do?"

Missy nodded her head. She was annoyed that Mrs. Bledsoe would talk to her that way. They'd hidden the pregnancy for the last six long months without talking about it behind anyone's back. Missy and Slimmy never said a word to anyone about it. They didn't even discuss it with each other. There might be other servants who knew the true story, but they also knew better than to say anything. It wasn't loyalty, exactly. It was more like a habit coming from the way they remembered the bad old days when telling tales could lead to serious beatings or even being sold away to strangers and being separated from loved ones forever. Mr. Whittington had never done that but they'd all heard about plenty of others who did. So, keeping quiet about whatever went on in the white man's house became a rule for survival.

When Ella had begun to have labor pains the day before, Mrs. Bledsoe sent the two farm hands and Joe's nephews home without any explanation. Nobody complained about being given an extra day of rest. The harvest was done and for the most part, they didn't care one way or another about the business of white folks. Missy had a few questions of her own but she would never have asked them out loud.

Before the birth, Mrs. Bledsoe planned to say that Eloise had gotten married down here to a fine young man, but her husband had been killed in a buggy accident. Missy had wondered how they would have explained her getting married without all the big hoopla that most white girls have about their weddings. Mrs. Bledsoe wrote long letters about who knows what and sent them up there to make the relatives think life in Alabama was as grand as she had expected it to be. Missy wondered if the woman made up stories. Had she written letters about a young man that didn't exist? If Ella was engaged and then got married, wouldn't the relatives wonder why they never heard of that fine young man before the groom was killed? Another thing was that if they'd showed up there with a baby then wouldn't it seem peculiar if they'd never heard of the groom and never heard the news of the blessed event?

At that time, of course, nobody knew about the baby being of mixed blood. Missy felt sorry for the girl. Her short life didn't have a lot of happiness in it. But then the girl wasn't a complainer either. She seemed to make the best of things. Considering the way her mother had treated her lately, Missy had to feel a certain amount of respect for her. Most of the young girls Missy knew would have been whining and rolling their eyes and making everyone around them miserable but Ella wasn't like that.

The baby didn't matter to Mrs. Bledsoe anymore. Nobody would even know the baby ever lived. The story was and always would be that Ella died after she fell from her horse. No one would know about the other horrible things that went on there that day. That was probably for the best. Rita Bledsoe declared it to be so, and Missy and Slimmy agreed to back her story. Even Missy recognized that it wasn't going to do any good to call the Sheriff about what the woman had done. It wasn't likely that she would ever do it again and she might even turn on Missy and blame the death on her. Mrs. Bledsoe wrote the date of Ella's death in the pages of the big black Bible but left out the birth altogether.

Missy felt bad that the girl had died in her care. Her guilty questions about whether her use of the willow bark tea had made the situation worse ate at her conscience. She finally decided that after everything was over, she would talk to Mona but she would also get up the courage to talk to the doctor about that too. She would not tell him about Ella and the baby, but since he already knew that she delivered babies for the black community, she could probably ask him because she wanted to know his opinion on the subject. Maybe he would give her some guidance. Maybe he wouldn't. She wanted to know more about how to use the willow bark or even the pennyroyal to make her a better midwife. After thinking on that for a minute, she felt much better.

Mr. Overmyer, the local blacksmith, who also doubled as the local undertaker, brought in a box to put the girl's body in. It had been a sudden call; he didn't have a proper casket ready, and there was no time to build one. The man that Mrs. Bledsoe sent told him that it didn't matter what kind of casket it was and so he figured it was for a field hand and brought what he had available at the time. He hadn't known it was for the Bledsoes' daughter, or he would have tried to find something more suitable. Joe helped him carry the empty box inside and couldn't help thinking that it wasn't very pretty. This was a simple box made of pine. It had the rough and unfinished look of having been made in a hurry. As crazy as Mrs. Bledsoe was about this daughter of hers, it made no sense to him that she would be buried in a coffin that was normally used for a field hand. Her daddy and her Aunt Catherine were put away in better boxes for sure. Miss Catherine had one that was lined in blue velvet to match the riding habit she was buried in.

Eloise Bledsoe wore ribbons and laces her whole life and now she was being put in the ground in a common pine box. The girl deserved better, at least in Joe's mind. Maybe Mrs. Bledsoe didn't have the money for a fancy coffin. That was a possibility now that Mr. Bledsoe was gone. But then, when it came right down to it, the person inside probably didn't care much. When you're dead, then one box is probably as good as another, he reckoned. Still, if it had been his child, he was sure that he would've carved her a box that was fitting all by himself, if he had to.

The day started out in the usual way for late summer in Alabama, with the flaming sun coming up and the heat and humidity building steadily as the morning wore on. The housekeeper, Slimmy, showed up and began her morning routine. She kept her head down and spoke quietly when she spoke at all. Word had been sent around that Miss Ella had fallen from her horse and died the day before. Some of the farm hands and a few of their Negro neighbors, who also worked on the farms close by, came to pay their respects and some brought in food but didn't stay long enough to eat any of it. The air was thick with tension and everyone could feel the awkwardness of the situation, even if they were not sure what brought the feelings on. They'd come in quietly and put their food offerings on the table and stand at the coffin looking down at Miss Ella for a minute, and then shake hands with everyone and leave. Not much was said and the mood was as black and droopy as the crepe bow that was hung on the front door.

Mr. Whittington and his daughter Amy happened to be in town and came and stood over the body for a short minute but shed no tears or said how much Miss Ella was going to be missed. They hardly knew her. They were polite, but it was obvious to Missy, who watched from behind a doorway, that the Whittingtons were anxious to get back into that fancy buggy of theirs and get on with their day. They had only come out of obligation and did not intend to stay to aid or comfort the girl's mother standing in the corner with her sad eyes and black dress.

The Reverend Mr. Jackson was there after noon, but spent most of his time sampling the food dishes one plateful at a time. It was obvious from the size of his waistline that funerals offered great opportunities to indulge his appetite as well as put a few coins in his pocket. He slapped people on the back and tried to make folks smile to lighten the mood, but it didn't do any good. He told Mrs. Bledsoe that Eloise was now residing in the arms of Jesus and that it was a day for rejoicing. Mrs. Bledsoe was not in the mood for rejoicing. She wanted the whole thing to be over and done so that she could leave. She told Missy that she didn't see any point in dragging things out any longer than necessary.

Joe said to Missy, "You know, being a preacher might be a good way to make a living. That preacher there gets to wear nice clothes and folks look up to him like he is somebody special. They's plenty of times that folks eat together on the church grounds after the sermons and the weddings and baptisms too. Some of those church ladies are real good cooks. I might could find me a woman if'n I was a preacherman. Yep, being a preacher might not be a bad thing."

She said, "Joe, what kind of foolishness you talking about now? You don't know nothin' 'bout bein' a preacher."

"Well, it don't look like a hard job, Sister. Think 'bout it. You jes' gotta say a few words or read something out of the Good Book and lead a prayer over the burial. Then you go back to the house and fill your plate with peas and corn and fried okrey and sliced tomaters, or maybe some of them chicken and dumplins or even some of that fried chicken. Then there's all them pies to choose from. I want me a piece of Miss Mamie's sweet tater pie. Anyway, I kin do dat, easy. I think it'd be a fine thing to stand up at the pulpit and tell people 'bout what dey should do and what dey shouldn't.

If I'as a younger man, maybe I could study up on the Scriptures and get into the preacher business myself."

She whispered, "I don't know what's got into people today. Even Mrs. Bledsoe is acting peculiar. And you? Hush yor mouth, Joe. Show some respect for dese troubled souls. What's da matter wif you?"

"I don't know, Sister. I was jes' thinkin' 'bout it, dats all. It was easier to think on dat stuff than to think about the real stuff dats going on. You right about the feelin' in here. It is peculiar. It's 'cause it's all a big fat lie. You know dat's what it is. You can feel the lies hangin' in the air. It makes it hard to breathe. I do hate lyin' pretty much more than anything else in the world...'cept killing. This here place is full up with both. Maybe I wouldn't want to be a preacher and have to deal with saving folks's souls anyhow. Maybe some folks's souls ain't worth savin'."

He stood there holding his hat in his hand and pretended to listen to the rest of what was going on. The more thought he gave it, the more he figured that he was too old to start thinking about changing his life that much anyhow. He reckoned that being a farmer and a handyman was what he knew and he might as well stick with it. Besides that, living the life of a preacher might mean he would have to give up the taste of the moonshine whiskey that he enjoyed sometimes. He also enjoyed spending a little time with the ladies once in a while. So he put the idea of being a preacher to rest and looked over at Mrs. Bledsoe to see what she wanted him to do next.

As soon as the grief-stricken mother decided that enough time for the visitations had passed, she kissed her daughter goodbye one last time, went over to Joe, and asked him to get some of his friends to help him carry the wooden coffin to the graveyard.

He was glad to have something to do. He rounded up Jack and Jimmy from out back where they were waiting for his signal. They shuffled into the house, picked the box up carefully, and carried it out the door and across the grass through the whitewashed gate of the picket fence surrounding the family burial plot. Two past overseers had planted family members in one side of the plot. Miss Ella was laid to rest in the Bledsoe half of the cemetery beside her father and her Aunt Catherine.

The weather had turned while they were waiting inside. The sun was gone and a soft misty rain had begun. It seemed fitting to Joe. Funerals and rain seemed to go together in his way of thinking. It was as if somebody up there in heaven was crying for the soul of the departed...or maybe they cried for the ones who were left behind.

He thought there should be another little grave in this plot, a tiny wooden box that held the bones of Miss Ella's son. He even considered coming back after everyone was gone to move the box from its spot without telling anyone. It seemed the right thing to do but with some people, it was hard to know what was right. No one had mentioned the child. Missy had not even asked him what had become of the tiny body. It was as if they were trying to pretend the birth had never happened. Joe knew not to interfere, so he didn't speak of it either, but he was sad to see the tiny baby separated from his mama in death. It didn't seem right somehow.

The preacher made his Ashes to Ashes and Dust to Dust speech and said a long and drawn-out prayer that ensured all the mourners were soaked to the skin. Joe and Missy said their "Amens" along with the rest before the small group began to break up.

The mud made a loud hollow-sounding splat as it landed on the wooden box. It didn't take long for the three men to fill the hole and mound up the top. The muddy water made tracks down the small hill like tears. The undertaker had carved a simple wooden marker and they planted it at the head of the grave but it didn't have the girl's name or any information on it. Joe said he would add those himself after everyone was gone. He and his friends collected their pay from Mrs. Bledsoe and left as quickly as they could. The sun came out again but the air was heavy and there was steam rising from the damp earth. The pitiful flowers hand-picked from the nearby fields and gardens were wet and falling onto the mud.

Ole Jimmy whispered to the men that he had a jug of white-lightnin' hidden out behind his shed. The men went to get it, and headed for the sand bar down at the river. They'd swim a little and sit around emptying that jug as well as the others that mysteriously appeared in a couple of other pockets. They hid their liquor from the womenfolk. The women said that drinkin' that stuff made them either mean or horny and they didn't want anything to do with them either way.

Chapter Seventeen

The next day, Missy and Slimmy did the laundry and cleaned the last remnants of blood stains wherever they found them. They stood around the boiling pot and stared at the flames licking the side of the pot. Neither said much. There wasn't much to say. Mrs. Bledsoe sent Joe to post letters to her relatives up north telling them about Ella's death and the fact that she'd be headed back home as soon as possible. She finished her packing over the week and on Saturday, she asked Joe to drive her to town to catch a train headed north. She told Missy, Slimmy, and Joe goodbye and said they could have anything out of the house they wanted. She said she was going home and would never be down that way again. She climbed into the carriage and never looked back. That part of her life was over and she wanted to forget it as quickly as possible.

When he got back from town, Joe took the food from the pantry and smokehouse. Slimmy wanted some of Miss Ella's pretty clothes and linens for her daughters. Missy took a small table that she'd always admired and placed it beside her own bed in the house she shared with her brother. The rest they left in the house for others to pick through.

Mrs. Bledsoe had taken Joe's offer of finding a buyer for the horses. He'd delivered them and given her the money before she got on the northbound train. Joe's part of the arrangement was stored in a coffee bag that he buried under the wood box in the kitchen.

The days passed the way they often did in south Alabama even in the wintertime. On one of those days, around the Christmas time after the bad things happened, Missy and Slimmy were sitting under the oak tree behind Joe and Missy's house peeling some late pears they'd picked out of the Bledsoes' little orchards. Slimmy swatted at a fly and asked, "You hear anything from Miss Bledsoe?"

Missy answered with a simple, "Nope, nary a word. We don't rightly know where she went. I reckon she's back up north with her kin folks havin' dem fancy Christmas parties with everything covered in snow like she talked about."

Slimmy accepted that because she hadn't expected to hear anything from her either. She emptied her dishpan full of pear peelings into the burlap bag they kept close by and gathered another double handful of pears to peel. They'd be putting them into jars that afternoon and had a few small apples to peel after the pears were done. They wanted to get them put up before the cooler temperatures came in January.

Slimmy didn't tell her cousin about her brother coming home the night before saying that Miss Ella was staring at him out the window of her bedroom as he passed by after his evening out with his friends. She'd figured he'd been drinking and his imagination was probably working overtime.

Slimmy said, "You think we orta cook these peelings down and make jelly outa the juice? We don't really need it none, do we?"

Missy said, "Well, we don't need the jelly for ourselves but it does sell good at the fruit stand. Let's get them apples done and we can look at how many peelings we got and maybe mix them together and make one batch of apple and pear jelly. We can strain it through a cloth and make it pretty and clear. I bet that would sell good. Joe can take a few jars to Mobile and sell them to the store there too. We made enough jes' on jelly last year to pay the taxes on the land and Joe said that was like gettin' free money."

Slimmy said, "Free money, my butt, he ain't the one doing all the work. Picking the fruit and peeling it and cooking it and straining the juice and putting it up in jars. Lordy, ain't that jes' like a man? Free money, huh? You kin tell him that when he gets his free money from dis here batch, I want me a share of it. You hear?"

"Well, now, I think he meant it was free because we got the fruit for nothin'. I gave you half the money we got from selling what we made together. Besides that, you didn't do the pickin' anyway. The kids picked it all. Mrs. Bledsoe said we could have what we wanted. It would be a sin to let all dat fruit just rot on the ground. And deys other people out there picking it up too. I sent Lizzie's kids out there the other week to pick up pecans. They got a whole sack full. So I reckon that pecan pie we gone have for Christmas was free too." She laughed but Slimmy didn't seem to think it was as funny as she did.

The house sat there, with its sad memories and whatever furnishings that were left. Piece by piece the items disappeared as squatters came and went over time. Nobody stayed for very long. It wasn't a bad house, but nobody seemed to like being there.

Ella walked in the yard and sat on the flat rock under the big oak tree and waited for something to happen. It was strange. She couldn't feel the dirt beneath her feet or the warmth of the big rock through her skin. She didn't know what she was waiting for, but didn't seem to have many more options in death than she'd had while she was living. She heard a baby crying but could not locate where the sound was coming from. She thought it was like being in a giant sized tent with gauzy curtains blocking the view of everything outside the walls, kind of like the one she had seen when the traveling preacher came one time and preached a revival. She spent a lot of time thinking about all the things that happened during her years of being alive and wondered over and over how she could have done things differently. She realized that much of her life had been totally out of her control but she also saw there had been things she could have changed. The first big change had to do with a certain stable boy and the things they should not have done on those lazy afternoons in the barn.

Joe, with the help of his two nephews, farmed his own plot of land and a little of Mrs. Bledsoe's too. Technically, he was still a tenant farmer but he had no idea where to send his payments so he never sent any. He figured that if somebody came by and told him to stop using the land then he would do it, but nobody ever came and so he used a bit of it as if it were his own and nobody ever objected. Missy and Slimmy canned some of the produce and they sold the extra from their roadside stand on the highway. The garden had always been good and they saw no reason to stop using it.

Missy kept working the hen house as though it were her own. She and Joe liked having fresh eggs and a chicken for the pot once in a while. They also kept a cow. Nobody had offered to buy her, and having her gave Missy and Joe fresh milk and butter for their own use and to sell. It brought them extra pocket money and nobody ever complained. Missy had her own coffee sack full of her collected wealth and it gave her a feeling of financial security she'd never known before.

Ella watched over them as they continued with their lives. She had no objections to their using the place or keeping the cow. Her mother had abandoned it all, and the extras it provided made their lives easier.

As a spirit, she wasn't able to touch them or communicate with them much. Once when one of the nephews fell out of the big oak tree, she went to Joseph and flew around him as fast as she could until he felt the cold breeze and got uncomfortable. She'd yelled at him and gone flying through his body and done everything she could think of until he finally realized something was wrong. He'd run around back and found the boy unconscious on the ground and took him inside the house. Missy must have felt the disturbance too. She came huffing and puffing from the garden and put cold wet rags on the boy's head until he came to. He had a bump on his head and it took a minute or two for him to get his breath back but he was all right.

Ella had felt so helpless. She wanted to be a part of things but couldn't figure out what to do. She wasn't able to communicate well and everyone seemed to be afraid of her when she made herself visible. After knowing Missy and Slimmy's families for so many years, it was frustrating to be separated by a veil so thin but so effective at blocking her efforts. Even though they knew her, they were so frightened by the idea of her being a ghost that they ran instead of trying to interact with her.

The Bledsoe place had played a big part in their lives but after Mrs. Bledsoe left, the biggest part of living for Missy, Joe, and Slimmy took place further down the dirt road with their own families and friends.

It didn't take long for the local folks to shy away from the Bledsoe place too. They said to each other that there was an eerie sad feeling around it. Rumors began to spread about the house being haunted by the specter of a tall young woman in a white dress. Some reported they'd heard a baby crying. Most said the ghost was Ella, the Bledsoes' daughter, who had died there after falling from her horse. Joe and Missy and Slimmy never commented but would give each other knowing glances whenever the topic came up in conversation. When they did discuss it with their families, it was done in hushed voices. They were not sure what they were afraid of but were taking no chances.

The Whittington Plantation continued to deteriorate. They never hired another farm manager. Mr. Whittington was so devastated by the damage to their home as well as the injury to his beloved wife in the big fire that he gave up farming and moved in with their daughter in Natchez. Mrs. Whittington never recovered from her injuries and died after a year or so, and her husband followed in a very short time. According to the townsfolk, he'd died of a broken heart. The daughter, Amy, and her husband inherited what was left of the place when her father passed away and eventually divided the land into small pieces that were sold off to the workers and other people one by one. Since their home was in Natchez, neither of them had any interest in farming the land or living in the big half-burned house ever again, so it was totally demolished.

Joe stood across the road that day, watching the big machinery tear the place down, and was reminded that houses, like people, eventually went back to dust. During his own lifetime, Whittington Plantation had gone from being one of the most prosperous farms in the state to being almost invisible. It was sad for some. But he and Missy had also gone from being slaves to having more than they'd ever dreamed of. His and Missy's little coffee sacks were full of cash in case of a rainy day and he didn't really want to go back. He was at peace with the present and looked forward to whatever came next.

A few years later still, during a springtime storm, a tornado swept most of their old house away and tore the porch off the brick house that held so many secrets. Joe and Missy moved out of their little house and in with their relatives down the road who continued to farm the land. They still used some of the planting techniques that had been taught to them by Mr. Bledsoe during his time as Farm Manager. It remained productive as long as they used it.

Eventually the younger family members moved on to other ways of making a living. One bright young man even became a doctor and settled in town to help any who needed his care without prejudice whatever their color or background. Missy was so proud that she had contributed to his education fund. It was like a dream come true.

Joe passed on in his eighties and Missy and Slimmy both lived to be nearly a hundred years old, with friends and relatives surrounding them with love and caring for them.

Once in a while over the years that passed, strangers would stop by the mercantile store or the gas station in the one-street town to ask questions about the abandoned house down the road. They usually wanted to know if it was for sale. There always seemed to be interest in old houses in the South, especially those made of slave bricks and full of old cypress or cedar wood and history. A few squatters still came and went but no one stayed for very long. The rumors persisted that the old place was haunted. The house sat there as a lonely reminder of the past, surrounded by weeds and deteriorating a little more each year. It appeared that no one in the white community knew the owners or how to get information about the place anymore, so it was considered to be a mystery.

Chapter Eighteen

1972

Army Captain Charlie Rivers and his wife, Melanie, were stationed at Fort Rucker, Alabama, the home of Army Aviation. Charlie liked his flying job with the Aviation Test Board and they both liked the area. They jokingly referred to it as L.A. or Lower Alabama. The post had the added benefit of being close enough to the Florida panhandle for weekend visits to the sugar sand beaches. Like many of the young families, they owned a ski boat and spent as many summer weekends as possible camped in tents on the beach with their friends. The guys went fishing, snorkeling, or water-skiing while the wives tanned on the white sand beach and played with their children in the shallow surf. They were happy there and often spoke of their hope to settle near Fort Rucker when the time for retirement came.

Melanie had relatives living in Troy, a small town north of post. She and Charlie made trips to visit aunts and uncles as well as her grandmother, who lived in an even smaller country village nearby. Being stationed there made Melanie feel connected and she was glad that her child could spend time with them too. She'd missed out on a lot of those extended family gatherings in her own growing up because her parents lived in another state and she only got to see her cousins and her grandmother once a year or less. Living near the relatives was giving her a chance to catch up and she was enjoying it. On any weekend there would always be a cousin or two at Grandmother's place and it was a great outing for a lazy Sunday afternoon.

The trip to Troy was less than an hour long depending on traffic and whether or not they stopped for a soda or a potty break for three-year-old Jenni. Often they took a route through Ozark, Alabama, to avoid the traffic at the main gate of Fort Rucker in Enterprise. One Sunday morning as they drove along, they watched for the old red brick house on the left-hand side of the road that they longingly referred to as their dream house. They looked for it every time they went out the back gate. They liked to make up stories about it. They'd even stopped a time or two to take pictures of the place.

There was something about it that tugged at them both from the first time they spotted it during Charlie's flight school days. With their tiny paychecks back then, they made jokes about the house being haunted and calling to them but they knew there was no way they could do anything but dream. It looked as though it hadn't been lived in for many years and would probably take a lot of effort to fix up to modern standards and a lot more money than he would make for years to come. During Charlie's first tour in Vietnam, he often daydreamed of getting back home, buying that house, and restoring it to its former glory. After he returned from his tour, they were blessed with a daughter and got sidetracked by life.

On that Sunday-dinner trip to Mel's grandmother's, curiosity got the better of them once again and they stopped to poke around a bit. They'd never seen any "Keep-Out" signs or anyone on the property to ask for permission to explore, so they pulled off the highway and followed a washed-out dirt road to an overgrown double track leading to the house, reminding themselves that they couldn't stay long, but they just wanted to see it again. Being there felt a little like trespassing but they did it anyway and enjoyed the naughty feeling.

The air around them crackled with excitement as they were both drawn to the place like ants to sugar water. They were fascinated by the double attraction as much as anything, rationalizing that there had to be something special about that particular house if it called to them both. Usually if one of them got bitten by a whim, the other was there to keep them sensible and put on the brakes before they did something foolish. But this place had them both in a tizzy. That was dangerous but also deliciously intriguing. Their eyes danced as Charlie drove the car carefully around in the tall grass. Both imagined that fate was drawing them in to make their dreams of owning the place come true. Each time they'd passed it, over the past few months, they'd talked about it for days. It was magic. It was a little spooky. It was amazing.

Charlie stopped, got out of the car, and told Mel to stay put until he looked things over to make sure it was safe. It didn't look or feel like a bad place, but he was very protective of his two girls. The door made a loud clunk as he slammed it harder than he'd intended. Mel felt a little shiver as she watched Charlie block his shoulders and take the first steps through the overgrown yard. She thought to herself, *Lord, please don't let him get bitten by a snake.*

Melanie got Jenni's socks and shoes back on, took her out of the car seat, and waited for her husband's signal that the coast was clear. She was tingling with excitement and it was taking all she could do to keep from following him to the house instead of waiting as she was told. She thought, *Do it right! Remember the ones that get whacked first in the horror movies are the ones that refuse to follow instructions. Somebody always tells them to stay put and they never do and they are always the ones who get eaten first.* She squeezed Jenni so hard that she said, "Mama, you are squashing my stomach and making my fingers hurt." She let go and said, "I'm sorry, honey, I am just too excited about seeing inside this old house."

"Why are you so 'cited? It looks like a broken house to me. Can Daddy fix it and make it look pretty again?"

"I don't know why I am so excited, Jenni-girl, I just am. We are not going to fix the house; we are just going inside to explore. It will be an adventure. You like adventures, don't you?"

"Yeahhhhhh, I like our aventures, Mama, can we go now?"

"No, baby, let's give Daddy a chance to look things over first. He wants to make sure it is safe for us to go on our adventure. Just hang on a few minutes more and then Daddy will say we can go in too. You help me watch for Daddy's signal, okay?"

Charlie went up to the house and walked around it first. He listened to the drone of the insects and felt the hot Alabama sun beating down on his shoulders and wondered what life would have been like when the house was filled with people and had life going on inside it. He felt certain the house was at least a hundred years old, maybe more if it really was from the days before the Civil War as he suspected. He wanted to find out more about the history but wasn't sure where to start. There had to be a story. The challenge was to uncover it.

After giving Jenni orders not to leave her car seat, Mel dug into her tote bag, got out the Polaroid camera, and took a picture of the outside of the place. She found a good camera angle and could see the front porch and columns as well as the kitchen in the back. The house really was kind of eerie but it was one of those places that also felt chock full of potential. It had a quiet kind of aura...more sad than scary. Mel claimed that she was sensitive to "bad vibes" and felt sure that she would have felt anything bad or dangerous right away. She told herself that the house was sad because it was in such bad shape and it would get happy as soon as someone, perhaps she and Charlie, could restore it to its former beauty.

The wooden parts of the house hadn't seen paint in years and the porches were rotted in a few places and sagging in a few others. The land surrounding it was dry and waist high with weeds and bushes. They would each need a good bug check that night to look for redbugs. Those nasty little red mites could make bites that itched for days. None of that mattered. Melanie squinted her eyes and imagined the lush green lawns, flower gardens, and the refurbished house full of lovingly polished antique furniture. She could almost smell the lemon oil. It was amazing what a good dose of overactive imagination could do when an old house was involved. There was history there. There had to be. You could feel it in the air.

The thrilling little shivers did nothing to discourage either of them. Some people are very susceptible to house fever and Charlie and Melanie were both infected even as they admitted the place would probably turn into a money pit. They were expecting to find the whole place eaten up by termites and wood rot.

The old house didn't appear to have ever had electricity installed or even indoor plumbing, which wasn't a surprise. The cornerstone at the front porch was marked 1848. Charlie took notes in a small spiral notebook to give him things to research later. He was hoping that this was a plantation house and he might be able to find out the name of the place if he gathered enough information. That made the puzzle seem even more exciting.

They'd already agreed that it was a bad idea to fall in love with an old house that needed so much work. They justified their actions that day by saying they were only looking around. It was an interesting place and they wanted to find out more about the history. They also agreed that neither of them was silly enough to believe they'd ever try to buy the place. They were a military family and could get transfer orders any day. But it was fun to look around and daydream a little. There was certainly no harm in a few daydreams.

Charlie finally motioned to Mel that it was ok to join him, so she plopped Jenni in her favorite riding place on her hip and followed her husband's footprints through the tall grass to meet him on the porch.

He lifted up his baby girl and carried her in his arms as they tiptoed into the gloomy hallway. It smelled old, but dry. Most of the doors stood partially open and hanging on rusted hinges. The wooden floors were terribly dirty and the corners were filled with leaves and twigs as well as large collections of mud and cobwebs. They saw the remnants of an inlaid design in the entrance hallway built from several kinds and colors of wood, making what appeared to have been a simple but very attractive pattern in the entrance hallway. There were a few small pieces missing and it was awfully dirty, but they teased each other saying that when "house-fever" hit a potential sucker, that sucker never saw the bad parts. Anything was possible in a dream and besides, they were only looking around. It was not as though they were foolish enough to do anything drastic like try to buy the place.

Charlie could not help but wonder where he'd ever find someone skilled in restoring inlay designs like that. He was very good with his hands and figured he could probably do it himself if he found the right books. He figured that it might be worth a trip to the post library to see what was available. There were bound to be books on the subject. There were how-to books on most anything.

There appeared to be many small rooms upstairs, but they didn't feel brave enough to climb the stairway even though it looked relatively sturdy. They weren't sure which rooms were parlors and which could be bedrooms because old floor plans could be baffling but they saw enough to know that the whole place could be beautiful with a lot of money, imagination, luck, and a healthy share of what Melanie's mama called "elbow grease." That translated into a lot of hard work. Neither of them had ever been afraid of hard work, but they did feel the need to be sensible. The whole idea was ridiculous. The whole idea was fascinating.

Charlie looked at Mel and said, "Don't you go getting any wild notions about our doing anything serious about this place, okay? You know there is no way we could do that."

She nodded her head and ran her hand over a piece of molding that looked to be hand carved. She began to smell lemon oil again.

"I know. We agreed that a person would have to be nuts to think they could do anything with this old house. But isn't it gorgeous, Charlie?" She pulled on a drawer handle of the dark wooden chest and laughed as it squealed open. It was lined with sheets of faded newspaper that were dated February 6, 1945. "From 1848 to 1945 and now it is 1972. Doesn't that make you tingle? Imagine what this old house has seen. You can feel the secrets oozing through the woodwork, can't you?"

Charlie said, "Okay, film crew, now bring in the camera for a close-up and cue up the spooky music we always play when the bogeyman is going to get somebody. Sheez! This really is beginning to feel like a really creepy horror flick." They both laughed.

Jenni was not sure whether to be scared or not, so she watched her parents and tried to decide if it really was a game or if she should be afraid. They were both being silly, so she decided that everything must be all right.

The nearly invisible girl in the white lace dress watched as the two strangers looked at all her things, touched the walls, and laughed together. She usually didn't like it when strangers came into her house. Some people were just curious and some were destructive. She especially didn't like it when the visitors wrote their names on the wood doorframes or on the walls. These people were different somehow. They seemed to genuinely like the house and even when they joked about it, they seemed in awe of the place. They talked about making the house beautiful again. Ella liked that idea. She liked the little girl too. She reminded Ella of herself at that age. The little girl looked up at Ella standing at the top of the stairs and wiggled her fingers gently. She didn't cry out or even speak. She just smiled sweetly and waved hello.

Ella decided at that very moment that if they wanted to, she would let this family stay in her house. She didn't want to do anything that would make them uncomfortable or afraid to be there. She was tired of being alone and there were questions in her mind that only living people could help her answer. This couple had been here several times and she wanted to get their help. She decided to whisper to them and hope they'd want to stay. So she waved to the little girl and smiled.

Mel and Charlie poked around in the outdoor kitchen and found an old two-tined cooking fork from a long time ago. Mel put it into her pocket. Ella grinned. A little gift would help to keep the house on their minds and was a small enough price to pay to hold their interest.

They joked about the outhouses that were leaning and about to fall down. They stuck their heads inside the doorway of one and saw the rough board seat with a hole carved into it. Charlie suggested that could be their new "potty stop" for their trips to Troy but Mel did not agree. Jenni wanted to look down inside the hole. They wondered why there were two of the privies but could not come up with any explanation except one for ladies and one for gents, or perhaps one was for the masters and one was for the slaves. They might never know but it was certainly food for thought.

After spending almost an hour soaking up the atmosphere, they realized they were going to be late for Uncle Cecil's birthday dinner if they didn't leave immediately. Before driving away they both stared at the house one last time and then looked at each other without saying a word. Neither of them really wanted to leave.

Chapter Nineteen

Charlie and Melanie spent the rest of the drive up to Troy daydreaming aloud about how they could make that house shine again and speculating about how much it would be likely to cost. They talked about the different kinds of wood in the entrance hallway floor and how to find the pieces they would need to repair the floor. Charlie wondered if there might have been some mahogany, but figured it was most likely cherry-wood that grew in the local area or at least had grown there at the time the house was built. They wondered about installing electricity and bathrooms. As far as they could tell, there was not a single closet in the entire house, so the rooms would have to be changed up a little to make room for storage. A modern family certainly needed a laundry room and they wanted more than one bathroom, and both needed to be inside the house. The detached kitchen had been an add-on out in the back to prevent fires from burning down the house in the old days. Mel remembered reading about that practice in a magazine but they'd want a more modern floor plan with an inside kitchen and a family room with a working fireplace for chilly winter days and romantic dinners.

Melanie dug her own spiral notebook out of her tote-bag and began to draw the floor plan as well as she could remember it. They could only guess at the upstairs, but it didn't seem too complicated from their view from the bottom of the staircase. They'd need at least two bedrooms and a bath and storage areas up there too.

Charlie even suggested that if "someone" were interested in the property, it might make more sense to tear the place down and start over. Mel disagreed loudly. Charlie gave in on that point because that defeated the whole purpose in both their minds, and neither would consider that to be a real option. They loved the idea of the place being very old and speculated about the previous owners and the history attached to the house. If "someone" were interested enough, they would have to find an architect to fix the floor plan to work for modern family life but still maintain the integrity of the old house. To their way of thinking, the house itself was the prize.

Melanie's family was full of builders and carpenters and they were sure one of the uncles would probably be able to do that for them at a reasonable price or recommend someone who could. It wouldn't hurt to ask them anyway. They might even know some of the history and it would be interesting to get their opinions if nothing else.

That afternoon after Uncle Cecil blew out the candles on his cake, Charlie mentioned their adventure to Melanie's parents and some of the other relatives while they sat around the big kitchen table. They were promptly told what a waste of time and money a project like that would be.

Uncle James said that he knew which house they were talking about and it would be a huge undertaking and a hell of a lot of work. He said that they should ask themselves why someone hadn't already rebuilt it if it were such a prize. That was a legitimate question. It was meant to be a bucket of cold hard reality thrown at them.

The negative talk did nothing to discourage either of the two dreamers. Love is blind and neither of them saw the problems. All they saw were the endless possibilities. They reasoned that old house was still sitting there because, obviously, it was waiting for the right people to come along. Maybe it was meant to be their house. They all had a good laugh.

Uncle James asked, "You aren't serious about that place, are you?"

Charlie said, "Awww no, we've stopped to look at it a few times and got carried away by the feeling of history there, you know? After I retire, we'd love to get an old house and redo it. Who knows, maybe it will still be there when the time comes. If not, I'm sure there are other old houses we could pick from to remodel."

Uncle Cecil said, "That place was been sitting there vacant even when we were kids. I can remember going over there with Daddy once to look at it sometime around 1930 or so. It was a pretty old house but it's gotta be over a hundred years old. By now it's probably full of rotten wood and termites. Daddy said those bricks were hand made by slaves back before the Civil War. You can see the hand and fingerprints from the slaves that made them. I remember one brick in the front of the place that had a hand print that looked no bigger than mine and I put my hand over the print and it fit perfectly. Some little slave kid my own age had patted that mud into the wooden form to make that brick. That made a real impression on me back then."

"I have to admit that it is fascinating for us. We're just curious. What do you know about the people that owned it?"

Uncle Cecil said, "I heard that it was once part of a big cotton plantation that had been there since well before the Civil War. I wouldn't even know who to ask. The local folks used to say that the place was haunted." He waggled his eyebrows up and down like he thought that that fact would freak them out. He looked silly and they were not freaked at all.

Mel thought that part was exciting. If the uncles thought saying it had a ghost was going to make them run from the idea of checking out an old house, they were both sadly mistaken. The idea of a resident spirit just added fuel to the fire for Melanie and Charlie. If there was a pill for house-fever, then somebody needed to call the doctor because they were both burning up with it that Sunday afternoon. Having the relatives tell them that they were wasting their time pushed them in the opposite direction too. Nothing makes a person want to do something faster than having a bunch of people tell them they shouldn't do it. Mel's stubborn streak was shining like a neon sign after her visit with her mother.

Chapter Twenty

On the way back home, they made a stop for gas and sodas in the little town closest to their dream house. They decided to ask the guy who pumped their gas if he knew anything about the abandoned house down the road.

The service station's owner grinned and wiped his hands on a red shop rag as he offered them a free glass of iced tea from the private gallon he kept in a rusty old refrigerator in the office area. He perched on a wobbly chrome stool and began to talk.

"That old house was once part of the largest cotton plantation in the county. The Whittington family owned the plantation, but the red brick house you are talking about was sold after the Civil War to the overseer after the big fire. None of their relatives live around here anymore. They all back up north some place."

He asked, "Are you folks interested in farming? That's prolly some good farmland. The place used to be famous for its cotton."

Charlie said, "No, not really. We just wanted to know the history of the house and find out if it was for sale or not."

The man slapped his thighs with both palms and said, "Well, guess what? You're in luck. A Yankee attorney came down here a few months back and give me a stack of business cards to hand out to anybody who seemed interested in the place. The family evi-dent-ly wants to sell the land. They must not have thought nobody'd be interested in the house because it's so old and didn't have no electrical power or indoor plumbing. They prolly figgered most folks would tear the old place down and start over or just use the land for farming. I don't know what they would be asking for it, but land is not that expensive these days so it might be a good deal for ya."

It took him a few minutes to find the stack of cards in his cluttered gray metal desk, but when he finally succeeded he told them to give that guy on the card a call if they wanted to know more. After they got back into the car, Charlie laughed nervously and swore to Mel that his fingers tingled when he first touched the card. She giggled.

Surely that had to mean something. The card was like a sign. The moon and stars were on their side and working toward making their dream come true. Charlie placed it in his wallet in a special place so it wouldn't get lost. He and Mel each had smiles from ear to ear.

Both of them held onto the new possibilities represented by that precious little white card the whole way home. There were no more games of pretending that they were not seriously interested. They'd be crossing a line by making the call to the attorney and they both recognized it. Neither even considered backing off. It wouldn't hurt to at least find out how much they were asking for the place.

They each tried to guess how much the land and the house would sell for and how much it would cost to restore it to some semblance of its original state. They had friends who recently built a new home and they wondered how it would compare to buying and rebuilding an older one. It was obvious there was a lot of work to be done but they were eager and ready to learn and thought that they could handle it.

Speculation and confidence seemed to play a big part in those daydreams too. Charlie figured that if it actually had been part of a real plantation then it was probably priced way out of their budget. The price would most likely be higher because of all that history. Anything antique would be likely to cost more, he thought.

Monday morning, they called the attorney whose name was on the business card. He told them that the descendants of the Bledsoe family, who owned the house and the surrounding land, lived in Pennsylvania and had for many generations. No one from their family had lived in Alabama close to a hundred years. They asked him if he knew any of the history about the house and he told them a lot.

The house had indeed been a part of the Whittington Plantation. The Whittingtons had owned a large and very successful farm that dated from the early 1800s. They had raised cotton and sugar cane and owned a lot of slaves before the Civil War. The brick house that they'd called about had been the home of the Farm Manager and was not the main house on the plantation. He said that he understood that the main plantation house had been damaged by a fire and eventually demolished and the Whittingtons never bothered to rebuild it.

Melanie listened to the conversation on the extension in the kitchen and tried not to interrupt but her mind was reeling. Farm Manager? Wasn't that the same as the overseer? Anything that hinted of being directly involved with the evils of slavery tended to make her feel squeamish in that modern time when so much effort was being put into racial equality. Her thoughts went straight to the ghosts that could possibly live there. Would they be the ghosts of the overseer or Farm Manager and his family, or was there some other more sinister story attached to the house? She was not thrilled with the possibility of a haunting if it involved murder and mayhem or the spirits of tortured slaves. It cast a negative note into the mix. Then again, she thought that maybe she had watched too many horror flicks and needed to calm her nerves.

She asked the attorney if he knew about the stories of the house being haunted and he laughed. He said he didn't believe in ghosts but, even so, he hadn't heard anything about any wandering spirits or scary stories.

He said that there were several pages of notes about the house in his file. Mel and Charlie heard him flipping pages and then he began to tell them the story. "The Civil War left the Whittingtons' place relatively intact because a Union general had used the place as a headquarters for a long time. When the family got back home after the war, they tried to put things back together, and hired back a lot of their own freed slaves as farm hands. During the time of reconstruction, they hired my client's ancestor, John Bledsoe, as a Farm Manager. He moved from Pennsylvania down to Alabama and into the small brick house with his family and stayed there for about eleven years or so. He did quite well and eventually purchased the house from the Whittingtons. Evidently that was quite unusual. John Bledsoe married a young woman named Rita Grayson and had a daughter named Eloise. John died from a stroke in the early part of 1882. His wife and daughter stayed there until the daughter was thrown from her horse in the latter part of 1882, and then Rita immediately abandoned the property and moved back to Pennsylvania to be with her family. She never returned to Alabama.

"The house sat vacant from that time on. There have been a few reports of squatters who moved in and stayed awhile from time to time, but basically the place has been ignored for all those years. The family up here in Pennsylvania wants to get it off the books, so to speak.

"The Bledsoes feel like it's been a kind of dark spot on the family name for generations. Evidently, John had been the politically active black sheep of the family, and his relatives even back then had not been happy about his running off to Alabama to join in the radical political upheaval at the time. They were a family of Quaker bankers and businessmen who tried to remain as politically neutral as possible about the slavery issues. There were a lot of Quakers in Pennsylvania in those days. The whole thing had been viewed as a shady patch in their otherwise sunny family history."

Mel asked him why the Bledsoe family would have been against their relatives coming south. She didn't understand why he would have been thought of as a black sheep.

He replied, "Well, I am no historian, but you have to understand that those were turbulent times up here. Most of the Quakers, or 'Friends' as they preferred to be called, were very much against slavery but things were building up toward war breaking out and being an abolitionist was getting to be dangerous even in Pennsylvania. They were pacifists. They wouldn't go to war but they did help in other ways. They often did things to help the slaves but they did it quietly. It has been said that they used to help escaped slaves get into Canada and whatever other things they could think of to aid the cause without taking up weapons. My client told me that our Mr. Bledsoe was quite vocal about his beliefs and it was beginning to interfere with the family's banking business. As much as they might have agreed with his feelings on the subject, they were also afraid for his safety at times. Many considered him a bit of a zealot and were probably glad when he left to take his zeal down south where it would perhaps do more good but also get him out of the line of fire. It was an embarrassment to both families. After he and the daughter died, his wife preferred to abandon the place instead of stirring things up by trying to sell it. She ignored the place for the rest of her life and her family pretty much forgot it even existed. The Bledsoes have paid the taxes on it and the deed is still in their name."

He sighed and began flipping pages again. "Ahhh, here we go. I was looking for a description of the house, since you asked about it.

"The property is for sale and is priced as forty acres of farm land, which does include a water well and a spring, and not for the value of the home. The water well may or may not be functional; you might consider having that checked out by someone who does that sort of thing. The house is included, however. It supposedly has three bedrooms, several sitting rooms, no electricity, and no indoor plumbing. I have to tell you that I have never seen the property. We sent an associate down there to check it out and take pictures. The pictures made the house look uninhabitable, so the family decided to price the place as though the house wasn't there. They figured most people would demolish the old place and start fresh with new construction." He also told them the amount that was being asked for the property.

Charlie didn't tell him their plan to restore the house because he didn't want the attorney to suddenly decide the house might have more value than they'd first considered. If it was included in the price then once they were given ownership, they could do anything to the place that they wanted to. He took notes in his spiral notebook and tried hard not to grin too widely. The price for the forty acres was very reasonable.

Mel asked if he knew anything about the Whittington house since it was probably large enough to turn into a Bed-and-Breakfast. The attorney knew nothing more about that place because it had no other financial connection to his client. Mel was disappointed but planned to do some serious research. She wanted to speak to the Realtor who worked with their neighbors when they were buying a home to see if the price for the land was in line with other properties in the area. She also wanted to see if there were any other houses like that for sale. Maybe it wasn't wise to jump at the first old house they saw, simply because they'd seen it as a dream. There could be something else out there that met their dreams without so much work and worry...and maybe at a better price. It couldn't hurt to see what was available.

Chapter Twenty-One

Mel and Charlie did contact the Realtor and looked at a few old farm houses but nothing had the aura or the special feelings of the Bledsoe house. To get a house with enough extra bedrooms for paying guests would cost them a lot more than they felt comfortable borrowing. That was the kind of dream that would have to wait until Charlie retired from the Army unless he got out of the Army early to make a career out of owning an inn. There were several Army Training courses that brought parents into the area for graduations and weekend visits and the troops living in the barracks had no places for friends and relatives to stay. A Bed-and-Breakfast was not a bad idea at all; in fact, it might be a very good one. Neither of them knew anything about running an inn but that wasn't really the problem. Charlie knew that he would miss the flying. He wasn't ready to become an innkeeper just yet. Neither of them was sleeping well and they knew a decision had to be made reasonably soon.

Charlie had to go to work the next morning, but Melanie couldn't stand not knowing the answers to the questions that plagued her. She packed her daughter into the car as soon as they finished their oatmeal to make the twenty-mile trip to see the little town once again. She was a determined woman on a mission to find out every bit of information available about the red brick house, even if it meant going door to door.

She went back to the gas station, but the man they'd spoken to days before wasn't working and the scrawny teen-aged kid who was pumping gas didn't know anything about it except that he and his buddies avoided the place because they'd heard it was haunted. He said that some of the military guys used the yard for parking with their girlfriends because it was a good place to watch the sun set. He told her that she'd have to come back when his uncle was there, and that Uncle Jack had gone to Montgomery to take care of some business and might not get back before nightfall. She refused to be discouraged.

After driving up and down the main street several times she pulled into the town library parking lot on a whim. She picked it as the starting place because her mother said that small-town librarians know everything that goes on in a small town. She hoped her mother was right.

The gray-haired lady sitting behind the desk looked up at them with her reading glasses halfway down her nose as they came through the door and asked if she could help them.

Mel smiled and said, "I was wondering if there's anyone here who could tell me something about that old house a few miles down the road. My husband and I liked it a lot and we're curious about it."

"Well, hon, y'all come on in. I'm Velma Griggs. I'm the librarian here. I can tell you a little about the place. What do you want to know?"

She had been sitting there alone in the building for most of the morning and was in a mood to talk. She invited Melanie to sit with her in the back of the room under the big windows with sunbeams shining down on the dark wood floors. They gave Jenni a big book full of pictures of puppies and she was happy sitting on the floor beside them.

Chapter Twenty-Two

Mrs. Griggs was born in the small town and had been a local history buff for most of her life. She knew exactly which house Mel was describing and it got her excited. She was eager to share. She grew up looking at the old house and had even spent an evening or two snooping around with her friends when she was a teen, hoping to see the resident ghost. She told Melanie that she and her own dear husband had looked at the old Bledsoe place themselves and had wanted to restore it at one point in their lives. They did a lot of research about it and had contacted the family up in Pennsylvania, but then her husband found out that he was sick with cancer and they dropped the whole idea to deal with his illness. He died a year or so later, leaving her to raise three small children by herself, so she never did think much about it after that.

Mel and Mrs. Griggs sat at the table sipping tea and nibbling on store-bought butter cookies that were shaped like little flowers. Jenni bit off the petals of the flower cookies one by one, holding onto them by putting her finger through the hole in the middle.

It was a fascinating and pleasant visit that did nothing to discourage Mel's interest in the Bledsoe house. If anything, it fanned the flames and made the fever grow hotter. She feebly tried to tell herself that maybe it was just a pipe dream. She didn't believe that for a minute.

Her mother had called the night before to say she was worried about the two of them getting caught up in that old house fantasy. She told them again how stupid it would be to "go off the deep end," as she put it. She certainly could not see Charlie getting out of the Army and changing their lives so drastically. She said the whole thing was a childish dream and they needed to realize that it was not a smart idea.

Charlie resented her mother's interference, and Mel wasn't happy about it either. They'd had to deal with her butting into their lives ever since they dated in high school. She wanted to be in on every decision they made and was convinced they couldn't do anything right without her advice and help. But there was always the chance that her mother was right about this decision. It was a huge step and they didn't want to make a mistake. But they didn't want to miss out on an opportunity either. Mel tried to get a grip on her overactive imagination but it was like holding onto a team of wild horses with a doggy leash. That morning at breakfast, Charlie had confessed that he was having the same problem. They'd decided to gather all the facts they could and go over everything but to make the final decision themselves, carefully, without being swayed by anyone else's opinions.

As they talked, Mrs. Griggs pulled out the bottom drawer to find a large manila folder. She pulled out a bulging manila envelope and dumped it on the desk top. There were lots of handwritten notes on a yellow legal pad and copies of pictures that had been taken a very long time ago. There was a black and white copy of a wedding tintype that was labeled John and Rita Bledsoe. The man was dressed in a stiff-looking black suit and a stiffer looking white collar and tie. He looked very much a businessman. The tall young woman was trying to look as dignified as her groom but there was a hint of a smile at the corners of her mouth and in her eyes. She was very pretty.

"Ohh, Mrs. Griggs, look at that dress. It is a wedding dress, isn't it? There are yards of ribbon and lace. It's very ornate with those flowers everywhere. I never gave much thought to Quaker wedding fashions of the 1800s but I have to wonder if that dress was what the usual Quaker bride would wear. I picture Quakers as being more plainly dressed than that."

Mrs. Griggs laughed. She said, "I'd never looked at that aspect of it and you are probably right. From everything I've read, Quakers were very modest and would not have worn anything so fussy. I would guess that dress is a bit over-done, even for that time...especially with that band of ribbon and flowers across her forehead. I don't think she came from a Quaker background. If I remember correctly her family was from some kind of Protestant faith. But she looks happy and a little mischievous, don't you think? I imagine they must have been excited about starting their new lives as a married couple, just like couples today."

"Well, she looks happy but he looks like his collar is too tight," Mel quipped.

They laughed and Mel handed her daughter another cookie. Jenni stuck her pointer finger into the center hole and bit off the first petal of the flower and grinned up at her mother.

Mrs. Griggs said "We probably shouldn't judge too harshly. We should remember that photography was in its infancy back then and the subjects may have to have held a pose for a long time to make it happen." Mel agreed.

There were other photographs of Mr. Bledsoe outside a bank with a group of other businessmen. There was one of him on a very large horse and one of him standing beside a huge barn. There was one with Rita sitting on a straight-backed rocking chair on a porch holding a small brown-haired girl on her lap. It was labeled "Rita and Ella." The young girl was decked out in a dress covered with lace and ribbons and she wore white stockings and high-buttoned shoes. Her hair was done up in long curls held by ribbons on each side of her smiling oval face. They looked happy.

The mother looked at her daughter with the same pride and love in her eyes that Mel hoped that Jenni could see when they looked at each other. It was easy to see she wanted to get down from her perch. Jenni had probably done the same thing a few times and it somehow made the people in the photo seem even more real and likable. She looked at the child in the photo closely and felt a sudden shiver run down her spine. It wasn't unpleasant, but it was strange. It was that feeling that some say means a rabbit ran over your grave. She wondered what it really meant.

There were also several photos of the house in Alabama as it looked back then. One picture was taken inside in a parlor and the family was gathered together on an old-fashioned couch. You could see the heavy draperies and more ornate furniture in another. It was quaint and old fashioned but it rekindled the flame of interest in the overseer's house.

Melanie grinned and asked if she could bring Charlie to see the photos.

Mrs. Griggs surprised her when she said, "Here, hon, you take it home with you and show it to him. You can keep the stuff. I am seventy-two years old. I'm never going to do anything more with this and my kids will throw the stuff in the trash when I'm gone. You take it. I hope that you and your husband do restore that old place. I think it would be a lovely home and after all, it is a part of our local history. I would like to see it preserved." Mel clutched the folder to her chest like a treasure.

She asked, "What about the old Whittington place, Mrs. Griggs? What happened to it? I kind of wish it were still around. That would probably make a great Bed-and-Breakfast, don't you think?"

"Well, now that is a sad story," she said. "I did some research on that too. After the War Between the States, the Whittingtons did move back home and they lived there for about ten or eleven years. The house was spared for the most part during the war. The records say it was used as a Yankee military headquarters for a while and even a hospital. They pretty much had to start over with the farm after the war though. Most of the plantations had a hard time getting restarted. Mr. Whittington hired this Bledsoe fellow from Pennsylvania and he came down here during Reconstruction.

"There were a lot of Yankee fellows that came down after the war to show the southerners what we had been doing wrong in the past and how to do it right in the future. I read in some of these papers that I copied that he was a Quaker who had some pretty strong feelings about slavery.

He was supposedly from a wealthy family and was well educated. A Yankee know-it-all!"

She gave a little sniff and a smirk and continued. It was obvious from her reactions that she thought Mr. Bledsoe was just another one of the carpetbaggers that claimed they helped to keep the South under control after that war.

She continued, "I researched old newspapers and found all kinds of stuff including documents and bills of sale for lumber and nails from the hardware store. That may not help you much but I thought it was interesting. The stuff is certainly more expensive now.

"The story was that the Whittingtons had a reputation of being fair and honest with their slaves and because of that, most of them came home after the war looking for work and the Whittingtons took them back for wages. It made sense, because they already knew the place and knew the way Mr. Whittington did things. They cleaned the house and barns up, put the land back to rights, and started over again. At one time the Whittington cotton and sugar cane were known for being the best in the state. The big house was supposed to be gorgeous. There is a newspaper picture of the outside of it in here somewhere. The newspaper articles said that that fellow Bledsoe was determined to regain that status and put things the way they ought to be."

She gave another little sniff and lifted her chin a bit when she talked about John Bledsoe. Her reaction was cute, but Mel got the feeling that Mrs. Griggs' research had not made her like the man very much.

Melanie wanted to like him if she could. She wanted to like him because she wanted his house, and everything she learned was making her want it more and more. She didn't have the same strong feelings about his being a carpetbagger. She'd looked up the term and found that it came from the cheap cloth luggage that many of those men had carried as they came down on the trains. The Bledsoes were from wealthy backgrounds so they probably came with leather trunks instead of carpetbags. Those men were usually political activists and slick opportunists and often made trouble wherever they landed. Mr. Bledsoe was more of a social experimenter. He wanted to do good things. It was a real shame that things didn't turn out better for him and the plantation.

"The Whittingtons had a daughter named Amy, who got married to a young banker from Mississippi. His family was quite well-to-do. During their engagement period, he was a frequent guest at the plantation. It looked like every time the young man came to call, the paper wrote an article about the visit. From what I read in the old newspapers and from the letters I found, those two kids were kind of like the prince and princess around here. I wish somebody would write a book about that place and get the family pictures together. Now, that would be a great coffee-table book for sure.

"There is a copy of another newspaper write-up in the envelope somewhere that tells about their wedding. It was one of the first in this area after the war was over and it looks like they did it up really nice. I remember the writer said good things about the dress Amy wore but I have not seen any photos of it. Evidently, her dress had belonged to her mother and came all the way from Paris, France, for her own wedding. That would have been a long time before the war, of course, but the article made it sound very elegant. No one in the area would have had the funds to pay for a new gown from Paris at that point, but wearing her mother's dress made it seem so special that no one cared about the lack of funds. It seemed to me that Amy was a baby born late in their marriage and the Whittingtons kind of spoiled her. That wedding would have been the biggest party since the old days and everybody who was anybody would have been there. The article alone took up most of the front page of the paper. After the big day, the newlyweds moved to Natchez.

"The banker son-in-law brought an infusion of money to the family and was able to help them start to rebuild things. Judging from the articles in the paper, everything was going fine for nearly ten years until there was a devastating fire. Nobody ever said what caused it, but a lot of the main house was burned beyond repair and then the barn caught on fire from a flying spark and several local farm workers were killed trying to save the animals. Back then they had a lot of horses and mules. It evidently was a very bad time in this town. There is a newspaper article that describes the fire in that folder too. It said that Mrs. Whittington was badly injured. It was terrible, I'm sure. Things had been going so well for them up to that point. It was really a shame.

"When I was doing all this research, there were still people living here who knew the family or knew of them anyway, so you might still find a few relatives. I remember talking to a couple of old black ladies who knew the story. It was interesting.

"Anyway, poor old Mr. Whittington seemed to have had a hard time of it after the fire. They started to rebuild but didn't complete it for some reason. There is a copy of a letter in there from the daughter to her father, telling him not to give up hope. It was given to me by one of the Whittington relations when I was doing my research. It was very sad.

"The daughter and her husband finally took her parents into their own home in Natchez and their Yankee Farm Manager was pretty much running the place by himself.

"Can you imagine? They still had the crops in the fields and somebody had to keep up with all that and keep the workers doing their jobs. The man was probably struggling to hold it all together.

"Then to make it even worse, John Bledsoe, their Farm Manager who lived in the house we were talking about earlier, died right after that. He apparently had a stroke or a heart attack or something. That is in another article from the local paper in the folder. Rita Bledsoe stayed on for almost a year, they say. I always wondered why she stayed on after her husband died. Then their daughter passed away too. She fell off her horse, according to the paper. Probably broke her neck. After that, I guess that the poor woman didn't have a reason to stay any longer. She packed up and left the house and went back up north to live out the rest of her life with her relatives in Pennsylvania. I was told that she just took what she wanted out of the place and left the rest to sit there.

"Those two old ladies said there were several black folks who lived near them that helped her out after John died. I remember my own grandmother talking about them. She helped me find the people to ask when I was investigating the house and the story but gosh, that was nearly twenty years ago. She told me that there was this one woman who was well known in the black community as a medicine woman and midwife for many years. My grandmother knew her. Her name was Missy Halcott. Granny said Missy lived to be nearly a hundred years old. Granny was the one who really pushed me into wanting to do something with the old house. We used to sit on the porch and she'd tell us all kinds of stories that Missy had told them. I was mesmerized.

"The Halcott family had all been Whittington slaves and then stayed on to work for the family for wages like so many of them did. They lived in a small wooden shack behind the Bledsoes' house and took care of the family as house servants until Mrs. Bledsoe left. The names are in the notes somewhere in the notebook. There was also a black woman who lived down the road who worked there as a scrub-woman and housekeeper. I remember her name was Slimmy or, well, they called her that anyway. I don't think I ever saw her real name anywhere. She was related to the midwife and her brother in some way, cousins or something. I knew her granddaughter. When I was doing my research, the granddaughter was still alive and we talked a lot about the family. She said that Slimmy and Missy had worked there ever since they were children...Missy had a sister that worked at the big house as a maid. I love history but talking to them and about them made the history come alive for me. I got all caught up in it. I always thought it would be a good book but I never started writing it. I took some notes, but not nearly as many as I should have.

"I wish now that I had recorded her stories on film or on tape. She was a smart old lady and I could have sat there for hours listening to her tell about the way things were back then, while we shelled a pan of peas or peeled a basket of peaches to make jam. It was more interesting to me than any movie or TV show ever could be. I was always willing to lend a hand in order to listen to the stories. The family wanted to sell the property to us but as I said, my husband got sick and then passed on so I never was able to do anything more about it.

"We lose so much history when the old ones die. I wish young people today were more interested in genealogy and history."

Mrs. Griggs was right. It was a fascinating story, but then Mel reminded herself that they might never get to do more than satisfy their curiosity or be able to go any further with the project either. That was a little upsetting. The more she learned, the closer she felt to the house and the people who had lived there so long ago...and the more she wanted to know. She had so many questions. Why did Mrs. Bledsoe stay in Alabama for nearly a year after her husband died? She also wondered about the daughter, Eloise.

It had been a wonderful morning. As the sun began to get high in the sky, Melanie finally gathered up her child and all their belongings, stowed the precious folder in her tote bag, and headed back toward home. Mrs. Griggs had managed to turn her distaste for the idea of the house belonging to the overseer into a matter of historic preservation. Those hard times may not be something to celebrate in our history, but they were important in many ways and deserved to be remembered so that we could learn something from them. That particular family seemed to be a good example of the system and not one that would cause embarrassment for anyone. It also helped that the story was downright fascinating. The Bledsoes and Missy and Slimmy seemed like real people to her now. She looked into their faces in the old photographs and wished there were some way to talk to them. There was a big picture of Mr. Bledsoe with a group of black folks on the front porch. Some were standing and some were sitting on the steps. She wanted to know if Missy and Slimmy were in that picture. She was betting they were.

Charlie and Melanie spent that week going over the notes and looking at the photographs and falling even more in love with the Whittingtons and the Bledsoe house, with all the people involved. On Sunday, they made a picnic lunch, packed up their daughter, and headed over to take another look at the place. They talked less and less about it being a matter of idle curiosity. Both agreed that it went deeper than that, but they wanted some answers before taking the next step of making an offer on the place. Mrs. Griggs was right. It was better than any movie or TV show. After getting so deeply into the story it would be very hard to walk away from the project if things didn't work out.

Charlie was very concerned about the questionable structural integrity of a house that old. Eighteen hundred forty-eight was a long time ago. He was surprised that the place was still standing at all. He wore his grubby jeans so he could poke around and do a little digging while they were there that day.

After laying out the two thick quilts in the shade of a huge magnolia tree for Mel and Jenni to sit on, he took his big flashlight and tool kit and headed off to investigate while Melanie read a library book to Jenni and watched her nap. Mel felt happy but couldn't shake the feeling that someone was watching them. She thought that she saw someone in an upstairs window while she put out the sodas, chips, and sandwiches for lunch. When Charlie joined them after his inspection, in between bites of ham and cheese, he told her that he found evidence of a fire in the wooden kitchen area but nothing in the main house was as wobbly or as rotted as he had expected. He didn't find any termites in the house structure either. That fact must go on the books as some kind of miracle. Most of the wooden portions of the house seemed to be made of cypress. The wood had the recognizable odor to it even this long after it was cut. There is an old saying that termites don't like cypress. Maybe it was true. There might be bugs in the out-buildings or the broken-down porches, but the house was amazingly clear except for some rotten wood and some damage that appeared to be man-made. They would get a professional termite inspection done anyway, but seeing it look so good did give him confidence.

The other critters didn't seem to notice what kind of wood it was made of, because he saw lots of spiders and lizards and even a long black snake under the porch. Mel freaked but Charlie said it was only natural since the critters had the place to themselves for almost a hundred years. They considered it home and the two humans were the ones trespassing. Mel agreed reluctantly.

Melanie and Jenni took a stroll around the house after lunch. Mel tried to imagine things the way they had looked in the pictures. The barn was gone but you could still see where it had been.

Jenni picked weedy little yellow flowers and held them out to her mother. Mel imagined the Bledsoe daughter, Eloise, doing the very same thing with her mother, Rita. They walked out back, crossed over the rows of a long-abandoned garden plot, and sat on a large flat rock beside the twisted remains of an old oak tree that must have blown down in a storm. It was amazing that the garden rows were still in place after such a long time. She'd never had a vegetable garden but seeing it there already laid out made her think it was a terrific idea.

Charlie joined them by the dead oak tree. There was a collapsed house and a fallen-down storage building nearby. It was sad to see any houses as neglected as these had been. He wondered what he'd find out there if he got a metal detector and ran it over the yard. There might not be anything valuable, but the bits and pieces of life as it used to be could be interesting, even if they had no monetary value. Melanie had cleaned up the old fork she'd found on their last visit and was now using it to turn meat when she cooked for her family. Using the old fork made her feel closer to the house and the family who lived there and besides that, it was exactly like the one her grandmother used every single day in her own kitchen.

Charlie walked the perimeter of the yard as far as it had been cut. He kept his eyes glued to the ground as though he expected some historical treasure to turn up with every step.

Someone had taken a tractor to it recently and the grass had been chopped down to ankle length, which was somewhat better than the high weeds they'd found on their first few visits. He was smitten and he knew that his wife was completely smitten as well. They wanted to know more. The thirst for knowledge was gnawing at them both. They questioned their sanity every day for even daring to consider buying a house that needed so much work. The possible cost of restoration should have been enough to scare them away but so far it hadn't.

Charlie said, "Okay, let's go over what we know. I'm still a Captain in the United States Army, and Captains do not make a lot of money. I am due to make Major sometime in the next year but we don't know when that will happen.

We could easily get ourselves up to our eyeballs in debt and in the middle of a massive reconstruction project and suddenly get orders for almost anywhere. Mooney and Faye just got orders for Germany. That could happen to us and I know you'd want to go with me. That would be a three-year tour of duty and I wouldn't want to go without you two. We couldn't afford to put this entire project on hold to move to Europe for three years. If that happened, and it could, how would we ever sell a partially finished house fast enough to make the move? Sometimes orders give us barely a few weeks to get the move set up."

Mel said, "Are you trying to talk me out of this?"

Charlie said, "No, I think I am trying to talk myself out of it."

Mel laughed and said, "Hey, I agree with everything you have brought up. It might be only a pipe dream after all. Maybe we should wait and do it after we're retired. The house has waited for a hundred years and if it's meant to be, then it could surely wait a few more until we can retire and settle down to do it with time for planning and common sense. I am just as caught up in the thing as you are, but maybe Mom has a point about our going off half-cocked. I hate to give her that much credit but we do have to be careful."

Charlie said, "Yeah, but somebody else as crazy as us could come along and snatch the dream right out from under our noses too. I'm not sure I want that to happen. There is something about this place that won't let go, you know?"

Retirement was a long time away. They wanted that house.

Mel handed a slice of apple to Jenni and thought she saw movement in the upstairs window again. She looked more closely, but didn't see anything except a bedraggled curtain. She decided that it must have moved in a draft from the old broken window. While packing up the quilt and toys to leave, she found a silver spoon that was intricately carved and pierced but tarnished black as if it had been lying there for a very long time. The handle bore the initial "B". It was another gift from a long time ago, like the fork. She smiled as she tucked it into the bag. Ella smiled too. An old spoon and a fork were not much but they were the only things she had to use as bait. She hadn't actually placed the spoon there but she'd seen it fall from the squatter's pillowcase as he ran away with the rest of the items he'd taken. It had been lying there for years. She simply led the young couple to the picnic spot under the big magnolia and let them find it on their own. She was confident that it would work. They were in love with the house and it wouldn't take much to get them to do what had to be done.

All restraint and common sense flew out the window. Charlie called the attorney in Pennsylvania the next morning and told him that they were interested in making an offer on the property. The man said that he'd mail them a packet that would include everything they needed to know including the instructions for filling out the forms.

Forty acres wasn't a lot of land for a farm, but for a military family, it was a lot of property to keep cut and groomed. They didn't want to be so tied down to yard work that they couldn't go to the beach once in a while. They might want to sell part of the acreage eventually. The money from the sale of the extra land could give them more to spend on renovating the house or even buying new furniture to fill it up.

The packet arrived a few days later and they went over the paperwork after dinner that same night. Both had given a lot of thought to the decision. They knew they were taking a big risk. If Charlie got orders they'd simply have to deal with it. They didn't want to be apart anymore. They'd already spent enough time separated during his two tours in Vietnam. The Vietnam War was winding down and a lot of the people they knew had been RIFFED...caught in the Reduction In Force that President Richard Nixon had started. That actually meant that they had been laid off from the Army. He had survived the RIF so far. Charlie was in a job that he liked and tried to have faith that he'd be stationed there for several more years. The biggest factor was how much they wanted that house, even if it was a crazy thing.

Charlie had been considering getting out of the Army and trying to get a civilian job at Fort Rucker. Mel loved the idea of "being home." Charlie seemed to like it too. There was a lot to think about and more than a few major decisions to be made. They were being blessed by fate or led down a garden path to ruin, and only time would tell which way things would end up.

After sleeping on it one more night to be sure, they filled out the offer to give it a shot. They offered a couple of thousand less than the price the attorney had suggested, licked the stamp, and drove it to the post office to send it on its way. Two whole weeks of going to the mailbox with crossed fingers nearly drove Mel bonkers. Both understood that the packet had to get to the attorney and then he'd have to go over it with the Bledsoe family and then get back to them, but they were anxious. If it was supposed to happen, then it would. If it was not meant to be, then they'd try to find a way to put it all behind them and get on with whatever came next in their lives.

The day the letter came from the Pennsylvania attorney, Melanie called Charlie at his office and opened the envelope while he was on the phone. They whooped and cheered together as she read that the offer had been accepted. The next step was to get a loan big enough to buy the place as well as give them money to do the restoration. That was scary.

Melanie let her fingers do the walking through the Yellow Pages to find a banker. They needed someone who had imagination and compassion to understand what they wanted to accomplish. She found it strange that all the banks bragged about how willing they were to loan money. She'd soon find out who was willing and who just talked about it on their commercials. She also reminded Charlie that Mr. Bledsoe's father was a banker and so was the young man who married into the Whittington family. That house had a lot of bankers in its history. She hoped that it was a good sign.

The first banker they talked to didn't even want to attempt the project. He told them straight out that a house that old was a huge risk and they didn't get beyond the first interview. He didn't come right out and tell them that he thought they were crazy, but he came pretty close. Charlie and Melanie were discouraged enough they didn't even stop for lunch at Burger King as they'd planned. Charlie dropped Melanie back home and went straight back to work. They were both upset by the encounter and Charlie began to worry again that they'd made a mistake.

Melanie refused to give up so easily. She got on the phone as soon as she put Jenni down for a nap and made an appointment for the next morning with the second one on her list.

The next bank had a loan officer who loved old houses. He understood their feelings and seemed to be more willing to listen to what they wanted to do. He laughed and said he'd been a victim of house-fever several times. There were framed photos of the three houses he and his wife had remodeled on the walls of his office. He joked about his wife hoping that somebody would come up with a cure for that illness one day. He knew the exact house they wanted to buy and confessed that he had walked around it a time or two, but his wife had immediately nixed the idea because it was too far from shopping in Dothan. He was excited by their plans and thrilled that he would get to see the house live again. He also suggested they have the house professionally inspected to get an idea of how much it would cost to fix it up the way they wanted it to be. He gave them a list of home inspectors and put a red dot by the one who had worked for him on his own three projects.

There were more papers to fill out. The inspections and the loan process took another month. The inspectors came up with a number that gave Charlie heart palpitations, but when he went over the list, he agreed that everything on it would have to be done to make the place livable.

Even though Charlie was very organized about keeping up with his finances, the loan officer called several times for more old tax forms or receipts for this or that. Charlie said that bank knew more about his finances than his parents. And it was true.

The loan was approved. Both of them were thrilled, scared, and excited all at the same time. They had never been so much in debt in their lives. The banker laughed and told them that most people feel that way when they buy their first house. Charlie told him that he would be thrilled under normal circumstances, but their house was a disaster and was going to take a long time to even become livable. The banker laughed again, patted him on the shoulder, and told him to put on his work boots and keep his eyes on the prize. He offered them a list of his favorite carpenters and other tradesmen that would help the renovation go smoothly. They were thrilled.

He asked if they'd mind if he drove out once in a while to watch it happen. Of course they invited him to visit as often as he wanted to, and he said that he would. The old house had so much potential. He was very glad to see them take it on and could hardly wait to see the end result. He offered a toast with their glasses of cola at the end of the closing, saying, "To old houses and those who love them!" They smiled and clicked their plastic glasses together.

Most of their friends and relatives seriously thought they might be losing their minds for going into debt. None of them knew exactly how much the debt would be, but they also thought it looked like the young couple was taking on a very big job. Mel's mother had an especially negative opinion and felt obligated to voice it more than once. Charlie's dad agreed to come for visits and help do some of the work to save a little money. He had worked as a carpenter while he was in college and would be a big help. Charlie appreciated the fact that his dad was willing.

Mel's father offered to help as much as he could with painting and sanding, but her mother still thought they had lost their cotton-picking minds. Mel told her that it was true. They were both cotton-pickin' crazy and it was all Whittington cotton and they might have to plant themselves a cotton plant somewhere on the property just to make it seem like they were restoring the place to its old purpose. Mama was not impressed. Charlie thought it was a fantastic idea. There were still cotton farmers in the area and surely one of them would part with a cotton plant for old times' sake.

The first thing they did was make arrangements with some of Melanie's uncles from Troy to meet them at the house to do a serious inspection. Two of them were kind enough to meet them on a Saturday and do another thorough inspection to see exactly what they were dealing with. Once again, Uncle James laughed at them and Uncle Cecil said they were nuts, the same things they'd said several months before at Grandmother's when they first told them about their being interested in the place. Charlie laughed and admitted they were probably right and asked them to help them figure out where to begin. The uncles took out their tape measures and screwdrivers and got to work, starting with the foundation. Uncle James had a friend who was a foundation man. He came out to take a look at it while they were there. The house was on piers, and it did need some major adjustments, but everything appeared to be doable.

They also had to replace the burned-out kitchen. Then there was modern plumbing to be added and wiring to be done since the old house never had electrical service. The floor plan had to be tweaked a bit. It turned out to be quite a challenge because there had never been any inside bathrooms or such modern conveniences as a laundry room. They also wanted central heat and air conditioning and closets...lots of closets.

The bedrooms were fairly large but they did add a bathroom off the master suite downstairs and made a bedroom for Jenni out of one of the downstairs sitting rooms, along with a hall bath for guests. They took out another little sitting room between two upstairs bedrooms to make a hall bathroom there too. It had taken several weeks to get the plans drawn up and approved before the loan was okayed so they were thrilled when the day finally came and the trucks and workmen arrived to make things begin to happen. Charlie and Mel held hands like teenagers as they watched. They took a whole roll of film to start a scrapbook of the procedure. Mel even took pictures of the old outhouses before the man knocked them down with the big bulldozer and filled in the holes. Charlie shook his head and said it was sad because that building was a symbol and knocking it down it meant the end of an era. He later decided to build himself a storage shed and cut out a moon on the door just to make it seem natural. Mel laughed at him.

They drove out every weekend to see what had been accomplished over the previous week. The project was not far enough along for them to start helping out but it felt good to see the things they had dreamed about start happening one nail at a time. Mel couldn't help but wonder what the Bledsoes would think of the changes that were being made to their old home. She hoped they would approve.

One Saturday they found their builder, Mr. Grantham, walking around the place when they arrived. There was usually no one there on the weekends when they came to visit the house.

He said, "Don't think I'm crazy, but I swear, I thought I heard a baby crying yesterday evening. I thought about it last night and decided that it might be a mama cat and some kittens. Maybe I'm a sucker, but I like cats, you know. We have two of them at my house. I don't want to do something to upset a mama cat or hurt her babies, so I came back out here to take a look around and see if I could find her and make sure that they're all right. We've had a lot of heavy equipment moving dirt around here and I just wanted to check things out. I hope you don't mind."

They didn't mind at all; in fact, it made them appreciate his caring attitude, but they also didn't find any cats. Mel still had the same strange feeling she'd had before, that someone was watching them. She went upstairs to the bedroom where she thought she'd seen movement in the window but didn't see or hear anything out of the ordinary there. She watched Charlie and Mr. Grantham talking beside the man's truck and decided that she must have imagined the strange happenings. She told Charlie about it after the builder left, but he started making noises and teasing her about feeling the spirits and seeing ghosts. She wasn't really afraid but she felt uneasy somehow.

They were glad to have had their builder give them the tour and talk about the progress they'd made. They got caught up on all that had been done and answered a few questions about their preferences on things that would be done in the future. It seemed even more like it was coming together after that. It gave them confidence that it was going to happen whether they were cotton-pickin' crazy or not. They were very excited to see the plumbing and the wiring go in. Those were two more important steps toward the completion of their dream home.

Melanie had fun picking out toilets, sinks, bathtubs, and other necessary things like faucets, towel bars, and toilet paper holders. She had catalogs all over their living quarters on post. She studied up on brand names and could tell a Moen faucet from a Delta or American Standard just by looking at it. She used a red magic marker to circle all the things she liked and then tore out the pictures of the ones she decided to buy. She began to hang out in hardware stores and make friends with carpenters, plumbers, and painters who also hung out in those places. She chose fixtures that had an old-fashioned look. She wanted the house to be modern but look reasonably antique. She and Charlie chose wide plank wood flooring for the rest of the house and they'd used the old floors as a sub floor but decided to preserve the inlaid floor in the entrance hall. They did have to replace quite a few pieces of the softer pine, but the oak and the pieces of darker wood that nobody could identify were in pretty good shape. The man who did the work was a true artist and did a wonderful job of using stain to match the color of the mystery wood. The inlaid design had the patina of age but was going to be beautiful.

It amazed everyone to realize how very old that wood floor was. The fact that it was still in reasonably good shape had to be a miracle. Even the construction people were surprised. It was almost as if the thick layer of dirt that covered it for so many years had acted as a protective covering. Like most people in the country, the Bledsoes probably used the back door more than the front, and the rumors of the place being haunted may have cut down on a lot of the traffic over the years as well. Once it was cleaned, lightly sanded, stained, and varnished, it was going to be a show-stopper.

Melanie remembered standing there one day and imagining the Bledsoe family walking into those very rooms and touching those same walls and door frames. It gave her goose bumps to think about it. She looked up and would almost have sworn that she saw a young girl standing there watching her from the top of the stairs. She dismissed the idea of course. Mel had always wanted to own a time machine. Her imagination must have been working overtime, that's all. She didn't mind. It was exciting. The house was steeped in history and she loved being there.

When the truck arrived to bring in the kitchen and bathroom items, Melanie was there and cried happy tears. Jenni clapped her hands together and squealed, "It's a potty, mama. It's our very own potty!" Even the delivery man who was carrying the potty had to join in the laughing at that one.

The house was eating up their precious free time. They spent so many weekends at the house doing as much work as they could to keep the costs down and to make the process go a little faster that they had no social life anymore, but it didn't seem matter to either of them. They'd learned a lot. Their close friends understood and some even offered to help. Charlie thanked them and said their support and understanding were all that was needed. The job supervisor gave them a list of things that he needed to be done and the dates that each chore had to be completed. He took the time to show them how to do each thing. They were eager to learn and did their very best. The carpenter was impressed and said he would hire both of them if they wanted jobs. They sanded and painted and spackled, and they discovered they liked the idea of putting their own labor into the house. Charlie called it "sweat-equity."

They also had an extra incentive. Baby number two was on the way and Mel wanted to get moved into the house before the new baby arrived. Four-year-old Jenni had shown them that they liked parenthood so much they wanted to try for a boy.

When they told Jenni that she might be getting a new little brother or sister, she told them that was okay but she would rather have a puppy. Her daddy said that she could have a puppy after they moved into the new house, and she seemed happy with that. She said that it had to be a white fuzzy puppy. Charlie and Mel told her they'd do their best and that she could pick the one she wanted when that time came. The animal shelter had plenty of puppies anytime you went there, so all they had to hope for was that they had a white fuzzy one on the day they went or that she would fall in love with whatever they had available at the time. She talked about the new puppy for days. She said he was going to be named Skipper because she liked the Skipper on the television show *Gilligan's Island*. They told her that was fine. New puppies and new babies all seemed to fit into the idea of living in the country, so they were happy with the total picture.

One particular Saturday, Jenni and Mel went to the house by themselves. Charlie had to work at the airfield for half a day and said that he would drive out to join them as soon as he got in from his test flight.

Mel was rocking out to Santana's *Abraxus* blasting from the 8-track tape player while hard at work, sanding in time with the music on the crown molding that would be installed in the living room. She felt certain she'd have it ready to stain by the end of that workday. Jenni played with her toys on the floor nearby. During the break between songs, Mel looked over to check on her daughter and was surprised to see a young woman wearing a sad face and a white dress standing behind Jenni watching her play. The teenaged girl was pale, almost translucent, and looked as if she had been crying. Mel was startled. She took a step toward them and the young woman instantly disappeared. That shocked her as much as seeing the girl in the first place.

She thought of every horror movie she'd ever seen and began to have regrets and scary notions again. The idea of the house being haunted had just gotten very real. She suddenly wished that they'd installed a telephone. There she was, pregnant, in an empty haunted house with her daughter and there was no way to call her husband for help. Then again, what would she tell him if she did call? Charlie didn't believe in ghosts. He would probably tell her that she was nuts.

Mel sat down on the wooden sub-floor with her child to calm her own shaky knees.

She said, "Jenni, are you getting hungry, baby?"

Jenni said, "Noooo, but can dolly and me have something to drink?"

Mel smiled at her looking back with those big blue eyes and poured her a cup of juice.

Jenni took a small sip, holding the cup with both hands, and said, "Mama, why was that lady crying?" Mel realized that they had both seen the apparition. It was good to know she wasn't just high on paint fumes.

Mel told the truth. "I don't know, Baby, did she scare you?"

"Nooo. But she was looking at me funny. She looked sad. When I saw her that other time, she didn't look so sad. That time she waved to me and was smiling. I think she is pretty. Don't you think she's pretty?"

Mel asked, "You've seen her here before?"

"Yes, ma'am. She was here that day when we had our a-venture. She was up by the top of the steps and she waved at me. I waved back at her and she smiled. Didn't you see her?"

"No, I didn't see her that day. I guess I wasn't looking in the right place then."

Mel tried to get back to work but couldn't get into it again. Her focus was broken and her hands had totally forgotten the rhythm of the sanding. Even Carlos Santana didn't help. Charlie showed up about one o'clock and she showed off her morning's work and accepted his praise.

They ate their picnic lunch sitting on the floor and Mel told him about the incident with the disappearing girl in the white lace dress. He looked at her and drew circles in the air around both his ears with his fingers to tell her that she was cuckoo. Jenni laughed. Mel told him defensively, "Jenni saw the girl too. In fact, she's seen her another time."

Jenni sat there nodding her head at him and blinking her eyes. "I did see her, Daddy. She lives here. This used to be her house. She was looking at me funny, like she wanted to talk to me, and her face looked like she had been crying. Mama asked me if I was scared but I wasn't scared at all. She just looked sad, not scary or anything."

Charlie looked like he didn't believe either one of them. He laughed and said they were scaring him. He said maybe Mama needed to check that juice they'd been drinking because it might have fermented. He also said they had a lot of work to get done so that the painter could get that molding up the next day and they didn't have time to be chasing ghosts.

They got the rest of the sanding done and wiped the crown molding off with a tack cloth and then applied the first coat of stain and wiped it off again. It was rich and dark and would be beautiful. It perfectly matched the stain they'd put on the fireplace mantel. By the time they came back the next weekend, the living room would be done and Mel could hardly wait to see it. It was such a thrill to think that one day this fall they'd be living here and lighting a fire in that fireplace.

They headed home after watching the sunset from their almost finished deck. Mel told Charlie about the kid at the service station saying that the military guys used to like bringing their girlfriends here to watch the sunset. Charlie waggled his eyebrows and said they could always put out the word that it was okay and charge them a couple of bucks to let them sit on the edge of the hill and make out in their cars. It would be a way to bring in a little extra income. Melanie playfully hit him on the arm.

He said, "Hey, every penny we could earn would go towards the cost of this fixer-upper, Babe! It could be as good as going to the drive-in movies like we used to do, remember?"

She hit him again but not very hard.

They packed their gear and headed on home after sunset. Charlie even did the drive-thru hamburger thing so that Mel wouldn't have to cook dinner that evening. It had been a very long but productive day. Mel silently promised herself that she would double up on veggies in their diets as soon as the house was completed. She hoped the Lord had blessed the man who invented fast food. It was a life saver some days.

Mel lay awake for a while that night wondering about the mysterious see-through girl that she and Jenni had seen. She tried to talk to Charlie about it but he started to snore in the middle of her story. Obviously, he was not overly concerned or maybe the poor man was so tired, he was worn out. Working all week at the Aviation Test Board and then using all of his time off to work on the house did not leave much time for rest.

Was it a ghost? Was it Eloise Bledsoe? She did resemble the girl in the photos. She wasn't sure that she believed in ghosts. Mrs. Griggs and the kid at the gas station had mentioned that the local people said the house was haunted. Maybe they were right. Maybe she and Jenni had met Eloise Bledsoe in person that day. Jenni wasn't upset over the incident, so Mel felt like she shouldn't be upset either. Maybe she would get the chance to ask some of the questions she had about the past. It could be almost as good as a time machine if that were possible.

She finally gave up trying to talk to her husband and bunched her pillow into a ball and went to sleep, trying hard not to keep asking herself over and over if ghosts were real and if so...had she seen one? Then the big question came to her suddenly. *If the ghost was real, then what does she want from us? Why was she there? Should we be worried? She seemed nice enough but how does a person know if a ghost is good or bad?*

The next day they both worked at the house but found it was very quiet. She and Charlie joked about the girl watching them and judging their work. Mel kept looking up to see if she would appear but nothing happened. She was disappointed on one hand and relieved on the other. At least now she knew that her feelings of being watched were real. She didn't seem to mind for some reason.

Jenni went looking around the house for her new friend but came back and reported that the lady she saw the day before was not there that day. She wondered where she was and hoped that she was not sad anymore. Mel was wondering where a ghost would go if she was not at her house.

Baby number two was growing quickly and Mel reached the stage where she was not able to do nearly as much of the hard work as she wanted to. She seemed to tire easily. She spent a little less time sanding and a little more time sitting on the floor with Jenni and her toys. One evening in March, they were sitting together on the breakfast room floor while Charlie was in the kitchen, pushing and shoving the new stove into the slot where it was supposed to have fit perfectly. She volunteered to help push but he told her that he didn't want her straining and taking a chance on hurting the baby or herself. He got some sandpaper and sanded the edges of the cabinets just enough to let the stove slide into place.

She and Jenni had the cabinet knobs and drawer pulls sorted out and she was about to begin screwing them onto the new drawers and cabinet doors. Jenni was muttering to herself and playing with one of the knobs. Mel had not been paying attention to what she was saying at all until she heard the words, "Daddy said Mama was cuckoo." Then she looked over her shoulder at her daughter and discovered that her four-year-old was having a conversation with their own resident ghost. Charlie got the stove into its space and turned around, saw the girl for himself, and gave Mel a disbelieving look. She gave him her own version of a see-I-told-you-so expression.

Mel looked at the young girl and asked her quietly, "Who are you?"

The spirit took a step or two closer and said very clearly, "My name is Eloise Bledsoe. You may call me Ella. This is my house. Why are you changing everything?"

Mel blinked a few times and tried to figure out what to say. She certainly didn't want to get the ghost upset. She'd seen ghosts in the movies go off on rampages and do horrible things. She said, "I'm Melanie and this is my husband, Charlie, and this is our daughter, Jenni. We like your house very much."

Jenni had no such reservations. She looked straight at the girl, shook her head, and said, "Noooo...this is our house. My mama and daddy buyed it and now we are gonna live here when we get it fixed up all pretty."

Ella nodded to the child, looked at Melanie's round tummy, and said, "Are you having a baby?"

Mel said, "Yes, it is due in late April or early May. We bought the house from your father's relatives in Pennsylvania, Ella. It has been sitting here empty for a very long time. We're rebuilding it. We want to turn it into a real home again. Is that all right with you?"

Mel thought that Ella might feel better about their being there if they asked her permission.

Ella moved across the floor and reached out as though to touch the new counter tops but evidently wasn't able to touch the surface without passing through it.

She said, "It looks new and shiny. Yes, it's all right that you live here. I saw you visit several times and I decided that it was time that I let someone stay. Your little girl could see me and she reminded me of myself when I was that age. But that was a long time ago."

She sighed heavily, "My mother never liked this house very much. She said it was much smaller and less fine than our home in Pennsylvania. But I liked it. I was a child when we came here, so I grew up in this house. I died here too." She turned around to look directly at Melanie with a strange sad look on her face.

Mel said, "I know. I read about it in the information that we got from the local librarian and your relatives in Philadelphia. I am sorry that you fell from your horse, Ella."

Ella blinked at her with a puzzled look on her face and said, "I didn't fall from my horse. Maggie loved me and I was a good rider." She laughed and said, "I would never have fallen from my horse."

Charlie stepped closer and said, "We were told that you were injured and then died from a fall from your horse. I'm sorry, we didn't mean to upset you."

"Oh, I'm not really upset. My mother would have told them that lie. That sounds exactly like something my mother would say. She wouldn't want anyone to know how I really died."

She continued, "I died having a baby. Well, the baby was born but after his birth, I started to bleed and Missy was not able to stop it. Missy did try to help me but there wasn't anything she could do. I remember hearing her say that I had a baby boy. I remember that she laid him on my belly and I was so tired and weak that I did not even open my eyes to look at him. I wish that I had. I remember that he felt so warm lying there. I never even saw his face. Missy wrapped him in the blankets that we made for him out of some flour sacks and put him in the bottom drawer from the big bureau in my room. I never got to hold him. I regret so many things. I never even gave him a name. I've thought about that so often. I should have made myself hold my child and I should have given him a big strong name. I hope that whoever raised him did that for him. I heard Missy say that he was a fine baby boy. I do hope that he grew up to be happy."

"Oh, Ella," Mel said. "I am so very sorry to hear that. I have tried to find out as much as I could about the house and about your family. No one must have known about that part. I never saw any mention of it in any of my research."

"No," she said, looking down at her shoes. "My mother would have made sure that nobody knew that part. She was ashamed of me, and my sin. I wasn't married. And my baby was fathered by a man of color. His name was Raymond. I never told anyone that before. I guess it doesn't matter. There is no way that anyone could hurt him now. He is probably long since gone too. He came through town and worked for my father for a short time after the big fire at Whittington. He left a couple of weeks before Papa died. He was a beautiful young man and very kind to me. I have wondered for years what happened to him. He said he was going to travel. He wanted to see the whole country, maybe even the world. I hope that he saw everything he wanted to see. I especially hope that he got to be a cowboy and slept under the stars."

She looked straight at Charlie and Mel as though she was watching to see how they would react to her news. Mel had tears running down her cheeks, so Ella seemed satisfied that they were not going to chastise her. She continued.

"Mother would have probably done or said just about anything to keep anyone in her family up north from knowing about the baby. She was very angry with me. We were supposed to go back up north to move into my grandparents' home after Papa died. She was so looking forward to that. I spoiled her plan to go back home. I have always thought that she wouldn't want to keep the baby because of his color. I suspect that she had Missy find him a home with a colored family that lived around here somewhere. That was probably best for him anyway. Missy would have made sure that he went to someone who would love him," she said sadly. "If I could not keep him, then I wanted him to have a good life with people who would accept him and not blame him for my sins."

She shook her head and shivered and then said, "I want to know more about my baby boy. I want to know what happened to him."

She looked at Mel. "I have looked and listened but I have never heard any news of him. I don't know who raised him or what kind of life he had. I hope that he was given to a good family and lived a good long life. That is all any mother could hope for, I guess. I remember that after he was born, I somehow managed to rise up to the ceiling and I could see all that was going on below me. Missy worked so hard to save me. I could see how worried and afraid she was. After a few minutes, I went past the ceiling and found myself going down a path of light that was filled with a soft mist. I could hear someone calling out to me. I couldn't see them clearly, but I think it was my papa and my Aunt Catherine. They told me to follow the light. I wanted to go, but I also felt like I was needed here. I tried to come back to be with my son, but somehow I got lost in the misty fog. By the time I found my way back here, my mother was gone. I wasn't surprised. She hated this place. I can't judge time the same way as I used to but Mother must have left for Philadelphia very soon after I passed on. There was nothing holding her back after that day. I could see that she took only her own personal things and left the rest to be picked over by anyone who passed through here. I hated to see strangers handling our things. I used to do everything I could to frighten them away. It was fun." She smiled.

"I don't know where my son was taken. I think that Missy and Slimmy must have found someone to nurse him. I followed Missy and Slimmy to see where they put him. I even tried to ask Missy once, but she could not see me or hear me. My little boy was only a few minutes old when I left him. If you are going to live here in my house, then please, would you be willing to help me find out what happened to my baby? It would mean a lot for me to know that he was cared for and to find out a little about how he grew up."

Charlie and Mel were both stunned. They wanted very much to help and agreed to do whatever they could to find the answers Ella Bledsoe sought. Even Jenni blinked her big blue eyes and nodded her head while looking from one to another. She understood that Ella was asking for help.

Charlie said, "Where should we start? The family members left in Pennsylvania didn't even know that part of the story. They wouldn't be able to help us find any information about a racially mixed baby boy born over a hundred years ago.

"Maybe the black community here would know more about it. If there are any of Missy's or Slimmy's relatives left in the town, then it would make sense to talk to them, I guess. We'll have to find them. It shouldn't be that hard if they are still around. I just hope they'll talk to us. Things are so weird right now with the blacks and whites not trusting each other. They may not appreciate us asking questions about their relatives."

Ella shook her head and said, "Why would it be like that now? Mr. Lincoln freed all the slaves and I thought that would make it better for everyone."

Mel said, "Well the slaves were freed but it didn't help them to get over the fact that they were slaves in the first place. Some of them still blame us white folks for the whole mess."

Ella looked confused. She said, "The ones I knew were glad to be free and didn't seem to have bad feelings toward us. Missy was almost like a mama to me. I certainly would have thought they'd have worked out all the problems by this time."

Charlie agreed. "Yeah, you would think so, huh? It is a very sensitive subject. We try to avoid making problems when we can. But I think we'll have to ask around and talk to a few of Missy and Slimmy's relatives if we can find them. The last name was Halcott. Mrs. Griggs at the library told Mel that there might be a few of them who are still around. We just have to hope that they have heard the story and know the ending."

Ella said, "Missy mentioned a girl named Ledbetter while I was in labor. Evidently the girl had a very easy birth and was up cooking breakfast the next morning. I wish mine had gone that well. Anyway, she might have relatives that still live here too."

Mel got caught up in the idea of helping the girl find out about her child. She had hope. Being pregnant herself made her sensitive to that kind of emotion. She called it a Mother-thing. The first hurdle was to find Missy and Slimmy's living relatives and maybe a family named Ledbetter.

She was afraid the black community in the small rural Alabama town was not going to be willing to discuss such things with strangers, even if it was supposed to be a time of easing racial tension. She didn't want to stir up problems for them or for her own family. She would have to be very careful of how she asked her questions. But first, she needed to find someone to ask.

Maybe, she could find a starting place if she went back to the library and talked to Mrs. Griggs again, she thought. She could always show her the picture album they had made that showed the renovation project from the beginning day to its present stage. Mrs. Griggs would probably be interested in the latest chapter of the story unless she thought Melanie was crazy. As much as Mel had enjoyed their visit that day, she didn't know the lady well enough to know if she believed in ghosts or not. Mel had never actually seen a ghost before seeing Ella. Nor had she ever told anyone that she had recently had a conversation with a ghost, especially when the ghost was asking for help. Even Charlie had thought she and Jenni were nuts when they told him about seeing Ella for that first time. He only changed his mind when he saw the ghost with his own eyes.

None of that really mattered. That poor girl deserved to know what had happened to her son and Mel was going to do what she could to try to find answers for her.

The next day, the carpenters were there to finish the large back deck. Mel approached one of the older black men and introduced herself. He told her that his name was Pinky Halcott. Paydirt! Maybe.

Mel asked, "Pinky, hasn't your family lived in this area for a long time? When I was doing research on the history of this house, I think I saw the name Halcott mentioned several times. Did your family have a connection to this house?"

He said, "Well, Ma'am, my family came from the slaves on the Halcott family plantation. Before that they was in Jamaica and in Africa before that. I don't know where they came from in Africa, what country, I mean. That part of the story got lost along the way. It doesn't matter much to me where they came from. I am sort of glad we ended up here, no matter how it happened. I'm thinkin' that me and my family are doing better here in Alabama than them long-lost relatives of ours left back there in Africa living in their mud shacks and having to go out and hunt up an antelope for supper. I got land of my own and I do carpentry work when I want to. We done come a long way from Africa. I ain't saying slavery was a good thing, mind ya, but we gotta make the best of the situation no matter how it came to be, don't you think?"

Mel said, "Well, I guess that is true, but just for the record, as far as I know, none of my relatives ever owned any slaves. In fact, many of my ancestors came here from Ireland as indentured servants and from what I have read, they were not treated much better. I think it was a horrible thing. But I have to admit that you guys are doing a fantastic job on this house and I am really glad that you are here too, no matter how it happened.

"I don't mean to get into your private business, but I am interested in everything about this house, and your family seems to be connected to it. Do you mind telling me about what you might have heard in your family stories?"

He laughed a little and wiped his forehead with his handkerchief.

"I don't mind one bit. I'm proud of my family and their history. Back before the War Between the States, the slaves sometimes used the last name of their owners. So, most all the slaves living on a small plantation could carry the same last name even if they were not really kin. The Halcott family place was called Rose Tree. It wasn't nearly as big as Whittington. It was a little place that backed up to Whittington on one side down by that road that goes to the old school house, and the O'Malley's place, called Shannon Oaks, was on the other side down yonder by the road going to Troy." He pointed off into the distance in both directions with his arms as he talked. "Old man Halcott must not have been too good at business. He sold off big pieces of his land one by one to cover his debts and got himself pretty much boxed in. My granddaddy said his granddaddy told them that Mr. Halcott gathered them all together one day and told'em that war was coming and he didn't have the money to last through it. So, he was selling off what was left of his place and all his slaves to the Whittingtons and then he was headed out west someplace. He said they was all real scared at first. My great, great grandmaw, Slimmy, and her cousin Missy and her brother Joe came with the sale. They was all just little ones at the time. They worked for the overseer in this very house from the time they was young'uns. Slimmy was a cook's helper 'til she got older and then she was housekeeper and cook for the last two families who lived here. Missy worked here too as a maid. With jes' the two of them, they did anything that needed doing unless it was heavy work. Then they called on Missy's brother, Joe, to help out as a handyman. I got an old picture album if you want to see it one day. They were some hard-working people."

Melanie was thrilled at that idea. She wanted to see how Missy and Slimmy and Joe looked. It was not quite as good as a time machine but it was almost as exciting.

"The first Whittington overseer broke his back falling out of a tree and died before my family moved here. The next one ran off during the war. Mr. Whittington and his family left to go someplace in Mississippi during the war. We heard some Yankee general come down here and took over the big house and just moved himself in like he owned the place. He told the Whittingtons they could stay if they wanted to but they didn't like being ordered around by a bunch of Yankees so they left. I don't know where they went but when the fightin' stopped they came back and started over. Uncle Joe told my granny that it was real hard putting the place back together and finding the workers and getting enough mules and stuff to make things work again. You know, folks don't like to think about it but the folks down here nearly starved to death during that ole war. Them was some hard times. Between the Yankees stealing the cattle and chickens and eating everything in sight, even the work animals were gone. Nobody had as much money as they did before the war, so I reckon it was real hard to get by. Then after the war that Yankee Mr. Bledsoe came to the place. Grandmaw Slimmy told my Grandmaw that they got on ok with him but that his wife was kinda uppity. Things rocked on for about ten years and they was getting along pretty good and then there was a fire up at the big house. Nobody knows how it started. But the place was near 'bout burned up. Grandmaw Slimmy said that Mrs. Whittington was hurt real bad and they took her to Natchez to stay with her daughter. She was burned on her legs and they never healed right. Grandmaw Slimmy said her legs drew up and was all crooked and she had to sit in one of them rolling chairs for the rest of her days. It wasn't long after the fire that Mr. Bledsoe up and died and then everything else kind of fell apart. But we Halcotts hung in here and did okay. Most of us are still around here. I reckon we never did like moving around too much."

He did seem to be proud of his family story. That was encouraging. Slimmy was one of the names given to Mel by Mrs. Griggs and she was also one of the two that Ella had mentioned when she told her story that day. The other carpenter was Reggie Halcott, and he was also related to Slimmy and Missy but wasn't sure of the exact connection. Mel was excited. Maybe it was fate stepping in again to help them. She would like to think that it was meant to be. Why else would it have happened so quickly?

Mel asked them, "Do y'all think that your ancestors would like the things we're doing to the house?"

Both nodded their heads. They both said they would probably like the new house a lot, but then Reggie reminded her that their ancestors had not lived in the house, that they had only worked there. He said Missy and her brother Joe had lived in that little shack by the garden that they'd torn down a few days before.

Mel told them, "I'm sorry, Reggie, I didn't realize it was your relatives' house. Did you tell Charlie before he asked you to tear it down? I am sure he would have found some way to save it if he'd known it had a special connection for you."

"Awww, no, Ma'am, we didn't need to save that old shack. It was rotten and nobody had lived in it for a real long time. I didn't think of it like that. It wasn't special to me at all."

Mel said, "Well, I can't help being fascinated by the history of this house and I wish I could find out more about everything that ever happened here. Mrs. Griggs, the librarian, was right. Real life is better than any book I ever read."

Reggie looked at her uncomfortably and said, "You might not want to get too carried away, Ma'am. There might be some things that you wouldn't want to know about. My mama always said that some old houses have old secrets and some of them might ort to be left buried in the past. You get to digging around and you might uncover something that you might not like."

Mel said, "That might be true, Reggie, but, please, I do want to know all of it. The good things and the bad. I think it's interesting to know how people lived back then, don't you? I know some of it or I think I do. I know about the Bledsoes living here and I know that they had a daughter named Eloise. The family called her Ella. The Bledsoe family still lives in Pennsylvania; in fact, we bought the house from them through an attorney. They told us that Ella died here and then her mother abandoned the house and returned to her home in Philadelphia. They said that she fell from a horse. We found her grave out back in the family plot."

Mel watched the two men squirming and saw immediately that they knew the whole story. She got excited. It was kind of funny to see two grown men looking sheepish and wanting to get away so fast. They began looking at the truck and then down at their watches...anything to end the conversation and get away from standing there. They said they were going to have to get back to work if they were going to get that deck finished by quitting time.

Mel didn't want to lose the chance to get that story out of them. If they left at that moment, they might never come back. That would be terrible for Ella and it could be disastrous for the completion of the work on the house too.

She looked hard at the older man and asked him straight out. "Pinky, what is the real story here? I have the feeling that there's a lot more to it than we were told. I think you know it, don't you?"

Mr. Pinky Halcott chewed on his full bottom lip for a minute and then pointed his calloused finger at her. "You done seen Miss Ella here, ain't you?"

Mel nodded and jumped in with both feet. There wasn't much point in hiding the truth if she wanted to get answers. "Yes, we saw her. We had quite a long conversation with her. She wants us to find out about her baby boy and what happened to him. She just wants to know his name and if he had a good life."

Pinky ran his hands over his nearly bald head and looked at the ground. "Awww, Ma'am, that ain't a good thing. You ought not to be goin' around talkin' to ghosts. I knew she was haintin' this place but I didn't think she would bother you folks. Me and my family been seein' her for years, but she never done nothin' bad or talked to none of us. We thought she only showed herself to black folks."

Reggie nodded his head in agreement. "That's why nobody wanted this place for so long. She was always hanging around here and we sometimes heard a baby crying too but we never could find nothin'. It was just a far-away sound on the wind. You reckon that was her baby? Ain't you scared to be here, knowin' it's got a ghost? I shore would be. You couldn't pay me to sleep in no house with a ghost."

Mel shook her head and said, "No, I'm not afraid of Ella. She's a lonely young mother looking for news of whatever happened to her child. She isn't here to hurt anybody. Maybe she's showing herself to us because we're planning to live here. She asked us why we were here and we told her about buying the place from her relatives in Pennsylvania. She says she is okay with it. She also seemed very interested in the fact that I have a baby coming. Maybe she felt a connection because of that. Do you know anything about what happened to her son? Ella seems to think that her mother would not have wanted to raise the child. She thinks Missy and Slimmy would have found a black family to raise him. I was hoping that you might have heard about it from an older relative or something. I'd like to be able to tell Ella how things ended up. Maybe if he had a family, I could even tell her that she had grandchildren or great-grandchildren, you know? She would be thrilled to know something like that, don't you think? Please tell me what you know."

Pinky ran his hands over his head from front to back in a nervous gesture, saying, "Awww, Ma'am...this ain't a good story. It didn't work out like that at all."

Reggie took a deep breath and started to talk. "No, ma'am, the baby didn't live here. He didn't live nowhere. I remember when I was a little kid, my grandmaw was talkin' about it one night. She said that Mrs. Bledsoe, that was the girl's mama, was all tore up after that girl died. She was screamin' and cryin' and sayin' that the baby killed her daughter. She said that Mrs. Bledsoe grabbed up that young'un and smashed his head and killed him dead. Missy was there to birth the baby and she saw it happen right there in front of her own eyes. She delivered all the babies for the black families around Whittington just like her mama had done. She'd told my grandmaw it was the most sorrowful day of her life. A lot of women died from having babies way back then because they didn't have the medicines that they have now-a-days. She'd done everything she knowed how to do but the girl couldn't be saved. They just said it was God's will, ya know? I reckon that pore old lady was still carryin' them bad feelings all the rest of her life even though she done the best she could.

"She said that Mrs. Bledsoe went plumb crazy. Missy's brother, Joe, buried the baby someplace around here. Grandmaw didn't know where. There never was a marker or nothin'. They didn't tell anybody else about the baby because Mrs. Bledsoe made them all promise they wouldn't talk about it because that young'un was half black and because Miss Ella wasn't married. Grandmaw told us Missy and Slimmy said nobody ever knew who the daddy was. They figured it had to be somebody who had worked here for a while and then moved on. After the slaves was freed they used to get a lot of workers who would come and stay for a short spell and then move on to someplace else. Ya gotta understand, it was a "freedom" thing, you know? For the first time in they lives they could pack up and move and nobody was gonna chase 'em down. Miss Ella went riding on her horse every day, so, they guessed it was one of the men who worked with the horses, but evi-dent-ly nobody ever noticed anything odd going on at the time.

"I ain't got no idea where to look for that baby, but he died the same day as Miss Ella accordin' to the story we was told. I'm sorry, Ma'am, I wish I could help the girl, but I don't know how." He plopped his old work cap back on his head and began to walk toward the truck, muttering about ghosts and spooky things goin' on.

"Thank you for telling me the truth," Mel told him as he wandered off. He reached in the back of the truck, opened up a plastic cooler, found himself an ice-cold orange soda, and popped the top. He downed the whole can in two or three big gulps. Then he turned around headed back to where he'd been standing. He took out his hammer and a nail and got back to work. Pinky put out his cigarette and joined Reggie to finish their job.

Melanie didn't know where to look either, but she could at least tell the girl Pinky's and Reggie's version of the full story and maybe she could help look for her baby. She'd waited a long time to know the answers. Mel wished the news was not so sad. The grandmother actually killed that child. There wasn't anything that could be done about it now, but grieving or not, the woman had gotten away with murder.

As they expected, Ella joined the family that evening. Melanie wasn't surprised to learn she'd been hovering nearby watching and listening while Pinky and Reggie told the story. She'd been crying again, but who could blame her? Any mother would cry after hearing terrible news like that.

She seemed to accept the fact that her mother did such a terrible thing as being perfectly logical. Mel was not sure she would have handled the news quite the same way. She'd have been much angrier. No wonder Ella hadn't passed over to whatever comes next. She wanted to stay here long enough to find her child. She'd had a lot of issues to work out here before going on to heaven or wherever she was headed and it had already taken nearly a hundred years.

Ella said, "I know you think what my mother did was horrible. It was. But my mother was not really an evil woman. She had a hard time living with the fact of her only daughter being with a man at all, and it only made it worse when the baby came and she saw that he was half Negro. She would never have understood that. Her instincts would have told her to hide it...or get rid of it. Things were different back then, I am sure.

"The man was my friend for the time that he was here. He took care of my horse and he was kind to me. I liked him and enjoyed listening to his stories about his life. He was young and full of dreams. I was lonely. We didn't set out to do what we did, but it happened and I knew that I could never tell anyone his name or he would have suffered for it. Even if my father was dead, the local white population would have hunted him down...not because I was anyone special, but because they would want to make an example of him to the other colored men in the county. I couldn't let that happen. He was a good man and didn't deserve it. I don't blame him for my situation. I don't think he knew anymore about what went on between men and women than I did. We were young and foolish but there was nothing malicious about him. God will not punish us for what we did. It was done in ignorance and innocence.

"My father was a Quaker and believed in equality of all races but my mother didn't always believe as my father had. She hated being down here in Alabama and hated living the life she was forced into by my father's job. Women were subject to whatever their husbands wanted back then. She was living a miserable life. After Father died, all she wanted was to go back to Pennsylvania. After thinking about it for so many years, I can't say I would have wanted to stay here if I were in her place. She was miserable.

"Even after we found out my child was coming, she stuck to her plan to go home. She was going to tell our relatives that I had been married to a young man from a fine Alabama family and my husband was killed in an accident soon after our wedding. I didn't like that idea very much, but my mother said it was a necessary sin. She said that I would be accepted by society if I was a young widow but that I would never be accepted as the mother of a bastard child."

Ella wiped her eyes and blew her nose on her handkerchief. Mel wondered if she had been using that same hanky for the past hundred years. Maybe things were different in the world of shadow where Ella was now.

Ella said, "I guess my having a Negro baby and dying was more than she could handle. She had told me over and over that God was going to punish me for my sins. She said God was going to teach me a lesson. I don't think she ever thought I would die from it though. Even she would not have believed her God would go that far to punish me. She was talking about us going home right up until the end. I know now that God was not punishing me at all. The baby was turned wrong for one thing and then the bleeding wouldn't stop. It wasn't God causing it. It was just the way things happened.

"Her grief caused her to do unspeakable things. But that is between her and the Lord, don't you think? We all have to face judgment, but I have seen enough to know that God is not nearly as interested in punishing us for our sins as he is in our learning from them. I do know that death is not the end. I am still here and have been for a very long time. I know now that I did the right thing. I have to find my child and I need to take him with me when I cross over to whatever comes next.

"I really messed up Mother's plans, didn't I? I wasn't surprised when you told me she ended up telling everyone that I had an accident. I wish that she could have thought up something better than my falling off my horse. I never fell off my horse in my life. My sweet Maggie was as gentle and well behaved as any horse could be. She would never have thrown me and I was a good horsewoman. I rode a lot. There wasn't much else for me to do. Oh well, I suppose she had to think of something reasonable. It would have been another of her necessary sins. She couldn't very well tell them that I fell out of a tree, could she?" She laughed at her own little joke but it was a sad kind of laughter that left them all feeling worse than before.

Jenni looked up at her with wide eyes and asked, "Did your mama let you climb trees? My mama won't let me climb trees, but I like to climb on the monkey bars at the daycare when mama leaves me there."

They all laughed and Charlie picked up his daughter and gave her a big hug. After all the sad talk about death and sadness, all she'd picked out to comment on was whether or not Ella had been climbing trees. Charlie said, "Ahhh, the innocence of children."

Melanie and Charlie didn't really know what to say. Charlie began trying to figure out where the baby could be buried. It was the only logical next step they could take.

"Ella, Pinky Halcott told us that Missy had a brother. He was supposed to have been the one who buried the baby. Where do you think he would have taken him? If we put our heads together, then maybe we can figure it out. There has to be a logical way to solve the mystery."

Ella shook her head and replied, "Joe wouldn't have been able to bury the baby in the cemetery with my father and Aunt Catherine. Knowing Joe, he probably wanted to. He was a kind man but he would never have disobeyed her. My mother would never have allowed it because of his color and because she was convinced that he had killed me. She probably didn't care what they did with him.

"Joe was a quiet man and a very hard worker. He was usually in the garden or doing some kind of job around the barn or the house. He chopped wood and drew water from the well. He helped Missy and Slimmy when they did the laundry outside in the big black pot in the yard. He also ran errands for my father and drove the wagon. He and Missy attended the colored church at Whittington. Maybe he would have taken the baby to the colored cemetery there, but I don't think so. He would have wanted to keep it secret, and to bury it there, he'd have to ask Reverend Jackson for permission. He would never have let anyone know about the baby because my mother would have given strict orders that it was to be kept a secret.

"Missy and Joe lived right over there by that stump of the big oak tree. They had a little house there, but most of it blew away in a storm a long time ago. You had those men tear it down when they were working on this house. They lived there most of their lives, first with their parents and then alone. It's hard to imagine, but a bunch of kids grew up in that little house.

"Missy got married when she was very young, but she came back home after her man died from a fever. She never remarried. She delivered babies for most all her life but never had one of her own.

"Joe never married. He was very quiet and shy around women as far as I could tell. Well, he was shy around my mother and me anyway.

"They shared the house and work, until the house was nearly blown down in another big storm a long time after all the bad things happened. Then they moved in with folks down the road. Missy moved in with one of her cousins and Joe stayed with one of his relatives whose wife had run off with a peddler some years before. I was here but I don't think any of them could see me. I watched and listened to them a lot. They never talked much about when we lived here. I think they all tried to forget that the whole thing ever happened.

"Sometimes people would move into this house for a little while. I never could get any of them to talk to me. If I showed myself, they got afraid and didn't stay here long. There were some who did things to the house. I didn't like them being in my house. You saw the writing they put on the walls and the carvings they made with their knives? I was always afraid they'd set the house on fire, either by accident or just to be mean. It got to the point where I would scare them off as soon as possible. After a while, nobody wanted to live in our house anymore because it didn't have those wires or the indoor pipes. That made it better for me. But it got lonely when Missy and Joe moved away. I haven't left our property since I got lost in the mist."

"Ok," Mel said, "I need to think about this for a while. Ella, we'll be back here tomorrow and maybe you could take me over to where Joe and Missy lived. I want to poke around. Maybe we'll find a clue there."

Ella looked at her with her translucent face plainly showing that she thought it was a waste of time because she had been wandering around on that property for a hundred years, but she nodded her head. Charlie and Mel gathered up their child and her belongings and left for their home on post. Mel wanted to study the copy of the plat they got at their closing that showed the forty acres of land around the Bledsoe house.

After getting Jenni to bed, they laid the plat on the table and looked at it carefully with a magnifying glass. They saw the garden plot between the backyard of the Bledsoe house and the place where Joe and Missy's house had been. Tomorrow Mel wanted to look at every inch of that area between the two places. She didn't know what would make a place special enough for Joe to choose it as a burial spot for a child, but maybe Ella would remember something.

Mel decided that on that day she needed to be free to wander, so she put Jenni into daycare after her preschool. Jenni thought it was a special treat. She asked if she could climb on the monkey bars and Mel said yes, but it looked as though it might rain, so she had a feeling the children would spend most of their day inside. Jenni seemed to enjoy being with her friends at school and Mel was glad of that.

Ella met Mel as soon as she drove into what would one day soon be their driveway. The two of them began their study of the land behind the old kitchen. Ella described it as Mel walked and looked at the ground as they went. Mel didn't know what to look for. They knew that no one had put up a marker but, maybe there had been a special bush or flowers growing nearby or maybe the dirt itself would look different because it had been disturbed. The grave itself would not probably be very large but the color of the soil might look different somehow. They didn't find anything. It was discouraging.

Mel finally sat on the flat-topped rock near the stump of the old spreading oak tree. Ella told her that the tree used to be beautiful. It had long limbs that were low and almost touched the ground. She used to ride the bottom limb like a horse when she was a child.

"Joe and Missy were younger then. Missy'd yell out the back door, 'You'd better get out of that tree afore you fall and break sumpin'.' I would laugh and make the limb go up and down even harder. My mother would usually see me from the window or hear the voices and send Slimmy out to collect me.

"My mother was always disappointed in my behavior. She wanted me to be a dainty young lady like Amy Whittington. I was supposed to sit up straight and be very still and speak softly. She wanted me to be thin and pretty with curly hair and lots of friends and beaus who begged for the pleasure of my company. Instead, she had a tall, plain girl with stringy brown hair that refused to hold a curl, no matter how many times Slimmy used the hot iron on it. I never enjoyed the girly things she wanted me to do. I much preferred sneaking off in a pair of my father's old breeches and riding my horse. Mother had beautiful riding clothes made for me but I was much more comfortable in my father's baggy old pants. She tried to make me change many times but finally realized that I was stubborn, and she decided that it wasn't worth the effort anymore and gave up. Another big disappointment. Then I got into trouble and had a baby. She missed my father so much. She was so miserable that I don't think she ever realized that I might be missing him too."

Mel understood having a mother who always seemed to be disappointed in her daughter's behavior. Mel, too, had hoped to make her mother proud of her one day, but so far everything she'd ever done had either been wrong completely or not quite up to her mother's high standards. So far, the only thing she had done right was to give her Jenni as a grandchild. Even her mother could not find fault with that.

She told Ella that she wasn't plain at all. Ella rolled her eyes exactly the way that teenaged girls still did. Some things had not changed in the past hundred plus years. Even Jenni was already learning to do that eye roll thing.

It was frustrating to not find the baby's grave that day, but the new refrigerator was delivered and installed and the movers were due to come on Wednesday. It had been a long journey but she and Charlie agreed that it was worth every bump and bruise they'd suffered over the past year. She was very excited. Melanie could hardly wait to have a family gathering and let her parents and Uncle Cecil and Uncle James see how the place had turned out. She and Charlie talked about having a big BBQ as soon as they got settled in.

For the next day or so things were hectic. Ella stayed out of sight for the most part but sneaked and peeked and Mel, Charlie, and Jenni saw her even if nobody else did. She seemed to be enjoying the whole spectacle.

She ooohed and ahhed as the new furniture was placed and laughed as Jenni climbed onto her big girl bed and pulled the covers up over her head. They finally got most of the boxes of clothes unpacked and most of the towels put away. Mel spent hours laying down shelf paper and getting the dishes washed and put into the cabinets.

Charlie and Mel were exhausted, but finally they were able to see it as a home. Ella was a little confused because it looked nothing at all like the home she remembered, but she seemed to like it. One night while talking to her mother on the phone, Mel stopped herself just in time before telling her mother something Ella had said about the indoor plumbing. She realized that if she told her mother their family had a personal relationship with a ghost from a hundred years ago, she would think they were totally weird.

Her mother would never have accepted that and Mel realized that it would be simpler to lie. It reminded her of Rita Bledsoe's necessary sins...little white lies that made things run smoother and avoided bigger issues. She also recognized that was another thing that had not changed much in the last hundred years.

The incident also made her realize that she hadn't told anyone about the ghost of Ella Bledsoe and somehow that made her sad. People probably would think she was whacko. It was a shame that they could not feel comfortable enough to share the story with their friends.

They went to bed early that evening because they were both still exhausted from the move. Mel lay there beside her husband and dreamed of a baby crying. Somewhere around ten o'clock, she woke up from the dream, with tears on her face and a wet pillow. She hadn't rested well at all. They really did need to find Ella's baby. It was important.

Later in the wee hours of the morning, she went into labor with their second child. Mel wasn't surprised. Ella was in a panic. She was terrified that something bad would happen to Melanie. Charlie said he would call Ella on the phone, but then remembered that she couldn't pick up the phone. It was too far to drive back and give her the news personally, so he told Ella that he would come the next day to tell her the news. Ella accepted that, but only because they couldn't figure out any other way to do it. She seemed to be confined to those forty acres as far as anyone could tell. Charlie was not going to leave his wife until he was certain that she and his child were all right.

They drove Jenni over to a friend's house on post and Charlie left to take Mel to the hospital. On the way there, her water broke and ruined the white leather seats and dripped onto the carpet of his 1973 Mercury Cougar XR-7. He was very sweet. Mel felt terribly guilty.

She gave birth at 10:10 that morning. Jenni had asked to name her new brother Christopher Robin like the little boy in the Winnie the Pooh books. Christopher was a good name, so they kept that part but could not see saddling the boy with a name from a storybook. Charlie was afraid it would cause him to be picked on when he got to be school age. Mel agreed.

They didn't want to name him after Charlie because it would have made him Charles the Fourth. Charlie said there had already been enough Charlies and it was time for a new name in the clan. It was lucky that both the grandfathers had Lee as their middle name. Christopher Lee seemed to fit and would satisfy both sides of the family. He was a little guy, only six pounds and one ounce, but he was perfect and had the face of an angel.

The next morning, Charlie went to visit his daughter and take her to daycare. On the way he told her that she had a little brother. She said that was okay, but he had promised that she could get a puppy. He told her they'd get her a puppy as soon as Mama and Christopher came home and got settled in. She seemed happy with it for the moment but as soon as Melanie got home, he knew that Miss Jenni would be wanting that puppy. After he dropped her at the daycare center, he drove all the way to the new house to tell Ella the news. She was there with her handkerchief full of tears until he gave her the reassuring news that Christopher and Melanie were both all right and he showed her a Polaroid picture of Mel holding their new son. She was thrilled. She flew around the room and laughed out loud and then came back to look at the picture again. He laughed with her. A year ago, he would have told anyone they were crazy if they'd said he would be driving twenty miles to tell a ghost that he had a new son. Now it seemed perfectly normal.

A few days later they brought their new baby boy home and Ella cried more tears of joy. She stood over his crib and watched him sleep. She said that she wished that she could hold him. Mel wished that she could too. Even without it, she was a good sitter for both of the children. Mel felt certain that she would call out if she saw anything that wasn't right. She told Mel over and over that she was so glad that she didn't bleed like she had done and that she was so very glad that she hadn't died. Mel and Charlie were pretty glad of that too.

Miss Jenni looked through the bars of the new crib at her new brother and said he was kind of cute. She said he looked like a baby doll except that he woke her up when he cried and he made stinkies in his pants. That made everyone laugh, so when her grandmothers asked her what she thought of her new baby brother, she repeated her observations and giggled and waited for praise when they laughed. Little Jenni did enjoy being the star. They would have to make certain that she got an extra share of attention so that she would not see the new baby as a threat. Mel managed to hold them both in the big rocking chair and sing the old songs she sang when Jenni was a baby. Jenni joined in and sang the words softly.

Down in the valley –
The valley so low –
Hang your head over –
Hear the wind blow.

Mel looked down and saw both her beautiful children sleeping with her arms around them. When Charlie came in and bent down on his knees to get in on the group hug, she felt whole and complete and so full of love. She wished Ella had been able to feel that with her child. That was one of the joys of motherhood.

The next day, Charlie took his daughter to the animal rescue center to look for her puppy. They found puppies of every color and combination of colors that anyone could ask for. Jenni had her heart set on a white fuzzy puppy and they had two white ones to choose from. One was a little girl puppy and one was a little boy from the same litter. Jenni sat on the floor in the reception area with both puppies jumping and licking and playing. Charlie wanted the little boy and Jenni said the little girl was the pretty one. He was not about to separate the two puppy siblings, so he had the lady put them both in the big cardboard box he'd brought along in the backseat of the car. He paid the adoption fees and got his discount coupon for when the time came for them to be spayed and neutered, and off they went toward home. Jenni was in her car seat but could reach the puppies. She giggled and played with them all the way home. As soon as they stopped in the driveway, Jenni climbed out of her seat. Charlie released the puppies and they took off after his daughter. It was fun watching them run and play together. The little fuzzy pups would not get very large but they seemed well suited to their new life in a country yard. The road was far enough away that he was not worried about the pups right now but he wanted to get the backyard fenced in as soon as possible to protect the pups as well as the two children. Ella smiled. She was enjoying their family. She was glad to learn that family life did not have to be as lonely and sad as her own had been. The truth was that Charlie and Melanie could not imagine life without their new friend. She fit into their life very easily.

After a few weeks, Mel and Ella took the children outside one morning to let Jenni play with the puppies and for them to get a little sunshine. Ella was shocked that Mel didn't mind her daughter going outside without a hat and actually wanted to let her get a little tan. She said that in her time, a girl child was never allowed to be outside so much and never to run around half-dressed. Jenni had on her blue and white flowered one-piece swimsuit and was playing in a small wading pool with a few inches of water in it that was warmed by the Alabama sunshine. She had so much fun splashing and squealing. The puppies climbed into the pool and splashed right along with her. It was loud but fun to watch.

Mel turned on the hose and let them run through the water stream and Christopher watched from his baby carrier in the shade of the big umbrella. Before going inside, she put the baby in the pool and dribbled water from her fingers over his belly as he laughed. He kicked and grinned and Mel hoped they'd both be tired enough to take nice long naps. Nap times were such blessings. There were still a few boxes to unpack and she wanted to get some flowers planted in the new flower bed by the front door.

On the following Friday, Charlie hired some men to remove the big oak tree stump. They were planting a new oak tree in its place as well as a few others scattered over the land around the house. Mel wanted a couple of pecan trees and they got a couple of peach trees too. One of the neighbors from down the road brought them a real cotton plant as a housewarming gift and Charlie planted it by the mail box. There was finally cotton on Whittington Plantation again. It seemed fitting somehow. They took a picture of it to go into the album. There had been a lot of changes to the old place, but it still retained the feel of being old fashioned. She couldn't resist calling her mother to tell her about the cotton-pickin' craziness of having cotton on Whittington Plantation again. Her mother laughed but seemed happy for them too.

The men brought a huge piece of digging equipment that looked like it was going to be loud and scary, so Mel kept the children inside while the men worked on digging out the roots of the big oak tree. Charlie stayed outside to watch them. He liked big noisy equipment.

Mel had just gotten the children down for naps when Charlie came running into the kitchen. "Where's Ella?" he asked.

"I don't know...probably watching Christopher sleep. Why? How's it going out there?" she asked.

"I think we found the baby," he said softly.

Mel ran to Christopher's room and told Ella the news. She followed as they went quietly out the back door and across the yard to the place where the large noisy machine was digging a very big hole. The big stump had been pushed over to one side and part of the roots were pulled out of the ground and stuck up in the air. Mel was amazed that the roots were so shallow. She would have guessed that they'd have gone much deeper.

Charlie and Mel stood on the edge of the hole looking down at a small wooden box lying at the bottom of the depression that was about four feet deep. Charlie jumped into the shallow end of the hole and picked his way through the root system so that he could carefully remove the box. He placed it up on the edge of the hole and climbed out again.

The driver of the big machine sat inside the cab and watched every move they made. Charlie had told him that the box might contain the bones of one of the previous owners' children and that they intended to move it to the cemetery if it was the baby. The man said he didn't care what they did as long as he got his hourly wage.

Unfortunately the big digging tool had broken the top of the box in several places. They could see the tattered remains of a piece of cloth but not much else. Mel looked up to see Ella standing off to one side watching. She was crying as they expected but she nodded to Mel for them to go on.

Charlie told the man that it was all right to continue with the project, and he cranked up the big machine and sunk its teeth into another part of the hole, freeing up the last of the matted roots.

Charlie lifted the wooden box carefully, walked it over to the back of his truck, and gently laid it on the tailgate with Ella floating over his shoulder watching and twisting her hanky in knots. She reached for the box and tried to remove a piece of the broken lid but her hands passed through the whole thing as though it wasn't there. It was frustrating for her. Mel felt sad because she knew how badly she probably wanted to touch her child.

Ella asked Charlie to please open the box so that she could see inside. With shaking hands, he slowly removed the pieces of broken lid and unfolded the deteriorating material. There was a little skeleton, perfect except for the skull that had been crushed in the back. The tiny bones were carefully arranged. Joe had done his best to make the little body look as comfortable as possible. The box was small and Mel could not help but think the skeleton fit into it like a baby doll would fit into a box at the toy store. Ella cried. The bones were so tiny, so delicate. He wasn't much bigger than Christopher. It was hard to think of how he had been born and lived for such a short time. Mel carefully folded the blanket's edges back over the remains and Ella told them that she had made the tatted edge on that flour sack blanket while she was waiting for him to be born. She said she'd never been very good at needlework but Missy taught her how to do tatting with a small wooden shuttle and that was the only tatted thing that she'd ever completed.

Mel understood that. She had several unfinished craft projects of her own packed away in the closet. Ella and Mel took the tiny coffin back inside to wait until Charlie was finished working.

Ella looked at the tiny bones and said, "I am so grateful for what you have done. I can't tell you how much it means to me. I had hoped that he grew up and lived a long life, but after finding out that he was dead, there wasn't much left to do except find where they had put him. I need to find his spirit. I have heard him cry but I think he was just as lost as I was."

Mel said, "Ella, finding him means a lot to us too. We fell in love with this house and wanted to know your story. Once we found out what had happened, there was never any other choice. We wanted to look for your child. Your family has come to mean a lot to us. We wanted to help you."

Ella said, "What do we do now? I suppose we have to bury him again, but where? I really want him to be with me but my mother was so against that. I don't know what to do."

Melanie asked, "Where do you want him to be placed? I certainly have no problem with putting him in the cemetery with you if that is what you want. Your mother has no say over it now."

"I want him with me. I don't care who knows about him. I would like it very much if Mr. Charlie could open up my grave and put him in the coffin with my own bones. Do you think he could do that?"

"We'll certainly ask him when he finishes with those trees. He is paying those guys by the hour, so we might have to wait until they leave. I'm not sure how they'd feel about seeing us digging up a grave. Finding the little one the way we did was an accident but digging up one in the cemetery is different. That might be something we need to do in private. We sure don't want to get into trouble with the law. Even though he died so long ago, I don't think it is legal to bury anyone now without a permit."

The children woke up from their naps and most of the afternoon was spent reading and playing with the puppies. Then they had dinner and spent time bathing both kids and getting them ready for bed again. They must have worn themselves out because even the puppies went to sleep as soon as they were put in their crates.

Charlie came in for a glass of water and agreed to open Ella's grave and place her son in her coffin. He'd expected it and was happy to make things right. In his mind, it made perfect sense for them to be together.

The tree stump crew left and Charlie came in to get ready for their nighttime adventure in the cemetery. The sun was going down but there was still plenty of light from the bright moon. The fence around the old cemetery was gone except for a few metal stakes and some twisted wire. The grave markers were also damaged. Charlie said that he was going to do whatever he could to repair and restore the old cemetery. Ella seemed glad to hear it.

Charlie and Melanie grabbed their shovels and carefully dug several feet down into the old gravesite working together until they found Ella's coffin. The ground was soft and it didn't take very long. She sat on the ground beside her son's tiny box and watched them intently as they worked.

The simple no-frills wooden coffin was very different from a modern one. The lid had been nailed into place but the termites had made a feast on the old wood. Charlie pried the lid off gently with his gloved hands, trying not to break the rusty nails or the old wood. Ella looked at her bones and commented that she was still wearing the same dress. Her aunt had sent the material for it for her birthday the year she died. It was made right before she found out that the baby was on the way. It had been the last new dress she'd ever gotten. Her folded hands held the tattered handkerchief that had soaked up a million tears. It had belonged to Missy. The tatted edging was loose in a few spots and the embroidered flowers had faded but it had held up well considering the use it had gotten over the past hundred years.

He carefully tucked the baby's little box inside the coffin with the bones of his mother. Ella watched and cried, which was perfectly understandable. Mel and Charlie had tears in their eyes too. She told Charlie that she wanted to hold her son, so he gently removed the little bundle of bones from the small wooden box and tucked it into Ella's bony arms inside her own coffin. She smiled then. She said, "I wish I'd been able to hold him before I died. I would think that new babies would feel so soft and warm."

Mel nodded and told her, "Yes, they do. A baby's skin is the softest and sweetest thing I've ever felt."

It was a strange and tender moment for all three of them. Charlie closed everything back up and shoveled the dirt back into the grave, and the two of them left Ella sitting on a rock beside her own grave. She thanked them again for all their hard work on her behalf and said that she needed some time to be alone with her son. The request seemed reasonable, so they left her sitting there.

All three had been on an emotional roller coaster for almost a year and the worst of it was finally over. Charlie and Mel left their ghostly friend and went inside to check on their own children. Mel made a fresh pot of decaffeinated coffee and they sat together discussing the strange but beautiful things that had happened that day. When they finally climbed into bed, they each slept better than they had in ages. The tension had finally been released.

The next day was Saturday and Mel made cheese omelets for breakfast. They were gathered around the big table in the kitchen and made it a festive time. They put their son's baby seat on one end of the table so that he could see everything that went on around him, and the four of them ate together as a family. Jenni tried a bite of mild salsa on her eggs and discovered that she liked it. She was happy because her parents ate salsa on their eggs and it made her feel more like a big girl. Mel was surprised but didn't stop her since the sauce was not very spicy. She figured that Mexican children grew up eating the stuff and it didn't seem to hurt them any. It was also a great way to get Miss Jenni to eat more veggies.

Ella joined them, with her baby wrapped in his flour sack blanket. She pulled back the corner of the coarse fabric to show them a beautiful little boy. He had skin the color of caramel. His big dark eyes were bright and shining and his pretty Cupid's bow mouth was smiling at them. He had the same kind of translucent body as his mother. She told them that she had found his spirit at the cemetery. He had been just as lost as she had been but now they were together.

Ella said, "I think I know how to get us both back on the right path now. The light has appeared to me again and someone is there waiting for us. Now that you found my child, I'm ready to go. I'm going to follow the light until we get to where we're supposed to be. Before I left for good, I wanted to tell you one more time that I really do appreciate all the help you gave us."

Mel and Charlie thanked her for the adventure and for making their home a special place. Having Ella and her story around made the house feel blessed. She had helped them be witnesses to history in a way that neither of them could have ever imagined.

Ella was smiling. She said the light was waiting for them and she didn't want to lose her way again. Charlie and Mel were very happy for them both. Her son was a beautiful baby. They understood that it was time for them to go. Jenni told her that she and her baby could stay at her house and live with her instead of going away. Ella said that she wouldn't be able to do that but she was glad that Jenni felt that way. She had spent enough years wandering around lost and alone. She gave them a sweet smile and disappeared. She and her son simply faded away. Jenni wanted to know where Miss Ella went and her daddy told her that they had gone to heaven. Mel believed that was true.

She looked at Charlie and said, "A little more drama would have been good."

He laughed and said, "Well, babe, I guess that's the difference between real life and the movies. Real life or death doesn't always have flashing lights and background music. She just went away but she was smiling and holding her son and she seemed to know where she was going this time. That's good enough for me."

Mel said, "I'm going to miss her. Knowing a real ghost was interesting. I liked her."

"Yeah, me too," he said.

Mel and Charlie and the children did miss Ella. They found all sorts of things that they wanted to talk over with the girl. Even Jenni would ask about her from time to time.

They lived in that very special house for three years before Charlie got orders for Germany. They easily sold it for more than what it had cost to rebuild. When they listed the house, the Realtor asked if there were any special stories about the place.

They carefully explained that the house had belonged to the Bledsoe family. They had a daughter, who had died after falling from her horse in 1882. They told her about the family burial plot out back. They didn't tell the most personal parts of the story. The house was beautiful and the history spoke for itself without sensationalizing it.

Some people believe that houses can store bad memories. That house was perfect. Any bad memories that were once attached to it appeared to be gone. It had been filled with love and happy memories and only good feelings during the time they lived there.

Over the years, Mel and Charlie often said they'd like to drive over to see the house if they were in the area. There was always a chance of being stationed at Fort Rucker another time. Mel went so far as to ask if they could buy it back if it were available. After all, it had waited a hundred years for them that first time.

Old houses have so much history and charm. It was too bad that the Whittington Plantation house burned down so long ago, but both Mel and Charlie were very glad they played a part in saving one little piece of its history. Mrs. Griggs, the town librarian who had helped so much in the beginning, drove out for tea one day before they left, and after the tour said that it was exactly the way she had seen it in her own dreams. She was very happy to see it restored and being enjoyed.

Charlie and Mel moved on to Germany for three years and their life together as a family continues to this very day. They never got stationed at Fort Rucker again.

Mel has to smile whenever someone tells her they don't believe in ghosts. People are entitled to their own opinions and she lets them keep theirs without going into it unless it's someone that she knows and trusts. Since her adventure with Ella Bledsoe, Mel has seen several other spirits and knows they do exist. Some were souls who lost their way and need a helping hand to get back on the right track. Some appeared to have chosen to stay back for some personal reason. But all of them were interesting and had a story to tell.

About the Author

ROSEMARY SMITH was a precocious child. Like many precocious children, her first word was "why?" She had imaginary friends, learned to read early, and drew pictures on everything she owned. Her mother bought newspaper end rolls to keep her from drawing on the walls. Her favorite pastime was looking through the World Book Encyclopedia and making up stories and poems. English and History were her favorite subjects in school, and even now she loves to add a bit of history to her stories.

She married her high school sweetheart and followed him during his Army career. When he retired from the Army and began his second career as a civilian pilot, they settled in south Louisiana. When she finally retired from her own Real Estate career, she began to write more seriously. She has four published children's books and one published novel and several others planned. She and her husband and their rescued cats still reside in south Louisiana, where the weather is hot, the food is tasty, and the people are warm and friendly. Her next book in progress is called *Finding My Own Bones* and she hopes to have it done by the end of 2015.

Books by Rosemary Smith: (available in paperback or e-book at www.amazon.com and other book sites)

Lizzie Walks On the Wild Side
Woody Gets Dunked
Lizzie Goes to Tea
Three Wishes for Maddy
No Earthly Boundaries

CPSIA information can be obtained
at www.ICGtesting.com
Printed in the USA
FSOW02n0538190815
9920FS